CAPTURING THE HEART OF THE ROCK STAR

KNOX BROTHERS OF ARBOR SHORES BOOK ONE

NOMI SUMMERS

Write from the Heart Books
P.O. Box 66202
St. Pete Beach, FL 33736

Cover Design by Elizabeth Mackey Designs

ISBN-13: 978-1-7332773-1-0

DEDICATION

To Anthony, and forever.

CHAPTER 1

"We have company," Shane Knox announced as he entered the warehouse. The rest of the band was already there setting up for practice, but Shane had been held up once again by thick LA traffic—a common occurrence when you live out in Malibu. Sure, it would've been easier for him to put down roots in West Hollywood. After all, that's where the rest of the band lived. But Hollywood wasn't really Shane's thing, and he needed to be near the water to keep his sanity. He never had been able to adapt to the hustle and bustle of the city, and he'd been in LA for nearly nine years. At least out in Malibu he could surf.

"Ah man, don't tell me." Sulley, the band's drummer, picked up his sticks and plopped down behind his drum set.

"You guessed it. He followed me in. He should be walking through the door in three, two …" Shane tossed his leather jacket on the faded brown couch that he'd crashed on one too many nights, and turned toward the door just as it slid open.

"Well, well, nice to see you gentlemen practicing." James Hunt, the band's manager, walked in on cue in his Armani suit. His slicked-back hair looked as if even a cyclone couldn't disturb it, and his bronzed skin made his pearly teeth a blinding shade of white in contrast. Had to be a spray tan. Then again, with all the money he made from the success of their band, Distant Union, he spent most of his time in St. Barts or on the golf course. Except today. Today, he had made the trek out to West Hollywood to see the band in person, and Shane knew that James only visited their dusty warehouse when he meant business. A visit from their manager was never good.

Shane sighed. This is not how he wanted to spend his Sunday.

"What are you doing here, James?" Jax, the band's bass player, asked without looking up from the guitar he was tuning.

"You know why I'm here." James looked around, as if in search of a place to sit, but the look on his face said nothing met his standards. He navigated his way through the equipment and cords strung across the floor. "You boys have a new song for me? Let's hear it." He stopped in front of Shane and waited with crossed arms.

The four band members shared glances and then all looked to Shane. As the lead singer, Shane knew he would have to handle James, as usual. "We're working on it."

"Working on it?" James repeated with an arched brow, one that Shane was sure had been waxed or plucked.

"I told you to stay off our case about new material. We can't be creative when we're being pressured. Like I said, we have some ideas we're working on." Shane's jaw tightened as he straightened his back and squared his shoulders. He couldn't stand the heat James had been putting on them lately. Truth was, they hadn't come up with new material in years, which made the whole topic a little … *sensitive*.

Distant Union hit it big seven years ago, just two years after Shane fled to LA to pursue his music career. At the time, he had just met his band after nailing an open mic night, and they were discovered shortly thereafter by James while they were playing a regular gig at a club on the Sunset strip. For the first few years, Shane wrote hit after hit, and the band topped the billboard charts on a regular basis. They were one of the most popular bands of their time, and their three hit albums had them touring to sold-out venues across the globe.

It was a whirlwind at first, and everything Shane had thought he'd ever wanted. But after a few years of being on the road and sleeping on the bus or in different hotel rooms each night, Shane had grown tired of the travel—travel that put distance between him and his new bride, A-list actress, Naomi Wilde. Shane had eventually caught Naomi cheating with her co-star when a film took her to the south of France for six months. They hadn't even been married a full year when the story broke and pictures of her in the arms of Brock Knight surfaced in every tabloid known to man. The divorce was over, but it had been messy. Shane's writing ability took the biggest hit. It was hard to write love songs when you'd lost your faith in love.

After he discovered the affair, he poured his soul into one broken heart ballad, but it tanked, and James made it clear that nobody wanted a song that had Shane's bitterness poisoning it. He was warned to come up with some fresh lyrics—lyrics that would make the ladies swoon like they used to.

"Let me put it to you this way." James took a step closer, but Shane's six foot, three inch stature still towered over him. "Either you come up with some new hits, or the label isn't going to renew your contract. Need I remind you it's coming up for renewal? They are breathing down my neck, and I'm getting tired of making excuses for you."

"We heard you loud and clear." Shane closed the space between them and peered down at his manager.

"I'll give you through the week, and I'll be back next Monday to see what you've come up with." James walked toward the door before he turned to add, "Oh, and Lori was able to get you booked on *The Aftershow* in New York a week from Saturday. It's just the PR you need to put you back on the map. We promised them you'd be debuting a new song on the show." He flashed a snide smile in Shane's direction. "No pressure."

"I'm leaving this Wednesday, remember? I'll be gone through Monday. We won't have time to come up with a new song by the following weekend." Shane walked away and began adjusting the microphone on its stand. "I have that wedding in Michigan. I told you about it."

"Do you really think this is a good time to be going on vacation? I just told you *The Aftershow* agreed to feature the band. That's huge. You need this publicity right now. It's already miraculous enough that you've managed to stay relevant when you haven't released anything in ages. The world needs a single. *Now.* How are you going to write that single if you're off gallivanting through Minnesota?"

"Michigan," Shane corrected him through gritted teeth. "I can't miss this, James. Don't act like you didn't know about it."

"It's fine, bro." Sulley walked over and stood by Shane's side. "Don't you worry about it, James. We'll make sure to have a fresh song. Shane can write from the road, and we'll learn it before the gig. Now get off our backs, will ya?"

"Don't let your band down." James shot a warning glance at Shane before disappearing out the door.

Shane picked up a half empty beer can and chucked it at the wall, the sound of aluminum on metal echoing throughout the warehouse. He didn't need the added pressure of writing a new song this week. Not when he had his best friend's wedding to attend and all the complications that would come with returning to his hometown.

"Maybe he's right. I shouldn't be leaving you guys at a time like this."

"Don't be crazy." Axel, the band's guitarist, walked over and placed a hand on Shane's shoulder. "You need to go. Besides, I've been looking forward to the break while you're gone. No offense."

"None taken."

"Yeah, I'll second that. I'd love to get outta this warehouse and spend some time with my family. The wife's been breathin' down my neck," Sulley added with a hint of his Scottish dialect slipping through. He'd been in the US since he was eight, but his Scottish roots had a way of coming out from time to time. Usually when he was excited or upset.

"What about you, Jax?"

"I booked a weekend getaway with my girl because I thought you'd be gone. I want to get some alone time with her before I'm stuck in this warehouse with you smelly guys all summer," he joked.

"Well, as long as you guys are cool with it, I need to get out of LA and clear my head. I'm getting tired of James pushing me to write something I don't feel. That's not why I started making music in the first place."

"The label just wants us to sound like every other band on the radio. They only care about what sells. They're taking the artistic freedom out of our music." Jax put down his guitar and folded his arms across his chest.

"Ah, the ole catch-22. To write whatcha love, or write what sells," Sulley chimed in. "Sometimes I miss the good ole days when we played small venues on the strip for peanuts. Times sure were more fun back then."

"I'll try to work on something new when I have some down-time in Michigan. I won't let you guys down." Shane stepped back up to the microphone.

"I'm not worried about it." Sulley slapped him on the back. "Now, let's get a quick practice in and get outta here. I'm tired of lookin' at all of yas."

Avery Cooke was up to her ears in wedding preparations, and on top of it all, her front desk receptionist had come down with a freak summer cold and had called in sick. How was she supposed to set up for tonight's chamber mixer, get this week-end's wedding guests checked in, and balance the duties that come with being the maid of honor for her future sister-in-law?

"Arbor Shores Resort, Northwest Michigan's vacation destination. How may I direct your call?" Juggling the phone lines was not something she had planned for today. "A tee time? Sure, hold please." She punched a button and set down the receiver. When would people learn they could call the pro shop directly?

She let out an exasperated sigh and smoothed her hands over her khaki shorts. She could handle this. After all, she'd been running this resort with her mother for the past three years since her father had passed away, and before that she'd worked at the resort for most of her life. Unlike her brother Dax, she'd even skipped college to work at the family-run resort; her father had been training her in hotel management right up until he died. An aneurysm. Sudden, and in his sleep. Nothing had been the same in Avery's world since that night, but she refused to let it slow her down. After her dad's death, she'd thrown herself into work, so she was used to the pressure that came with hosting events; she usually thrived on it. But this weekend wasn't just a typical wedding and the anticipation had her nerves on edge.

"Hey, Ave." Rylee Benton rolled her housekeeping cart to a stop in front of the front desk. "I just finished my rounds."

"Aren't you a sight for sore eyes. I'm glad you're here."

"You look like you could use some help. I've got some free time before my shift at Ripples starts. Put me to work."

Avery and Rylee had been close friends since they were young girls. Growing up, they were inseparable, until Rylee left for New York City just after high school to pursue a career in ballet and they'd lost touch. But Rylee recently returned to Arbor Shores, a single mother of an eight-year-old boy, and no ballet career to speak of. Rylee was the hardest working woman Avery knew, yet somehow, she always held a cheerful demeanor. Avery knew her friend was struggling to get back on her feet, so she had given Rylee a job cleaning at the resort a few days a week for extra income. Right now, she'd never been so happy to see her best friend.

"I'm going to take you up on that," Avery said, making her way around the front desk with an oversized basket containing a bottle of champagne, two flutes, a dish of freshly cut strawberries, and dark chocolate covered local cherries. "If you could place this in cabin number one, you'd be doing me a huge favor. Here's the key. I want it to be a surprise when the lovebirds get here."

Even though the bride and groom lived in Arbor Shores, they were staying at the resort for the weekend. It would be easier to have the entire wedding party on the property, and they had friends and family coming in from out of town whom they wanted to spend time with.

"Will do. What time are Dax and Leila arriving?"

"They went to the airport to pick up Leila's cousins, but they should be here soon." Avery tried to act calm as the phone rang again. She quickly made her way back around the front desk. "Arbor Shores Resort, how may I direct your call? ... Hold, please, while I transfer you."

Avery looked up and noticed Rylee had her head cocked to one side with a look of concern on her face. "What? Why are you looking at me like that?"

"I'm just worried about you, that's all."

"Worried about me? I'm fine." Avery began pulling reservations from a folder and lining them up on the desk. Rylee hardly looked convinced, but Avery couldn't blame her. She wasn't even sure she'd convinced herself.

"Listen, I know this place is your life, but this is your brother's wedding weekend, and I want you to enjoy every moment."

"This place isn't going to run itself, Ry." Avery shot a look at her friend.

"All I'm saying is I'd like to see you have a little fun. It seems like all you do is work lately."

"You're one to talk!" Avery half laughed, and for the first time all day a smile tugged at her cheeks.

"I'd just like to see you let loose, maybe date a little, get out of this resort every now and then. This weekend is the perfect opportunity." Rylee leaned in and brought her voice to a whisper. "And since a certain someone is coming back to town for the wedding, I was thinking—"

"Don't even think about it. Dating is the last thing on my mind, and I'm especially not interested in *him*."

A sly smile spread across Rylee's face. "We'll see."

The phone rang again, and Avery flinched. Was it the sound of the ringing or Rylee's words that had her on edge? "I have to get the phone." She motioned toward the basket. "Cabin number one. Thanks a bunch."

Avery dismissed her friend and the burning comment that was still ablaze in her mind. This, no doubt, would be one interesting weekend.

CHAPTER 2

*S*hane rolled his rented convertible to a stop at the red light and looked around. Not a thing had changed since he left Arbor Shores nearly nine years ago. It was early summer, and the town was already filling up with tourists from downstate who fled north on the weekends to enjoy the popular coastal lake town and all it had to offer. As small as Arbor Shores was, it sure drew a crowd from Memorial Weekend to Labor Day—the height of summer in northern Michigan.

Beyond the stoplight, the glistening blue waters of Lake Michigan welcomed him, with the town attraction, Ripples Bar and Grille, perched just steps from its sandy shore. Ripples was packed, as usual, and an outdoor band filled the afternoon air with tunes for the crowd that had gathered on the patio over-looking the beach. On his right, Callahan's town store was flooded with tourists. That's where he'd gotten his first job bagging groceries when he was sixteen. He wondered if Old Man Callahan was still alive. He'd have to stop in before the weekend was over and say hello. Shane watched as families filtered out of the storefront carrying beach supplies and char-coal, children with swim floats in tow headed for the beach.

Lucky kids. Did they even realize that these summer days at the lake would someday be among their best memories?

The sun hit the water at just the right angle, and the glimmer of the lake caught Shane's eye. As bad as the timing of this weekend trip was, he sure couldn't wait to jump into that cool water. It would be a refreshing change from the salty Pacific he'd grown used to out in Cali. As a well-known rock star, he didn't get much downtime to take weekend vacations, and everywhere he went people flocked to him. Finding peace was something he'd given up on long ago, so a part of him felt relieved to pull into his hometown where he'd hopefully get some privacy. Yet another part urged him to hightail it in reverse. Wouldn't it be easier just to leave than to face all he'd left unfinished long ago?

He'd secretly been dreading this trip since he'd received the news that his childhood friend Dax was getting married. Shane hadn't been in Arbor Shores since he was nineteen, but Dax had asked Shane to be his best man. He had to come. He owed Dax that much.

It was Dax that saved his life the summer after graduation, and Shane always felt he owed him something in return. He knew that someday he'd find a way to thank his best friend for that fateful night when Shane had taken his father's dune buggy for a weekend camping trip with the guys. Dax and the others had stayed back at the campsite to start the bonfire, and Shane took off to get one last ride in before the sun dipped into the lake. When nightfall came and Shane still hadn't returned, Dax went looking for him and found him trapped under the overturned cart, unconscious and bleeding from his head. He'd pulled Shane from the buggy and carried him a full mile back to the truck where they'd sped to the hospital. Shane had lost so much blood from his head injury, the doctors said much longer trapped upside down, and he wouldn't have made it. His adoring female fans generally went crazy over the scar above his right eyebrow, but for Shane it only served as a constant reminder of just how much he had to be grateful for. And how much he owed to Dax.

A double tap of a horn from the car behind him alerted Shane that the light had turned green. How different it was to be home. In LA, he would've been flipped the bird for missing the changing light. He gave the man in the car behind him a wave and turned right, speeding north up the evergreen-lined coast to where the resort stood about a mile outside of town. With the top down, he was able to feel the cool June air on his face as the early summer sun fought to warm him. He took the corners at top speed, enjoying the winding road that snaked up the coast.

He slowed at the familiar sign and turned left into the resort. He followed the long drive, past the landscaped entrance with its manicured green lawn and tall pines that guarded the outside world from the oasis that awaited beyond the gate. Set atop a large hill overlooking Lake Michigan was the massive log cabin-style main lodge. The resort's private golf course rolled down the coast on the left, each tee box providing a stunning view of the westernmost Great Lake that ran the length of the property. At the bottom of the hill were cabins spaced out along the shore, with the Beach Club in the middle of it all where guests spent their days under private cabanas around the pool or finding solace from the sun inside the Beach Café. A wave of nostalgia hit him full in the face as he took it all in, memories fighting for space in his mind. He pushed the thoughts away as fast as they came and rolled his car to a stop in front of the lodge.

Was he ready for this?

"Checking in? What's the name?" the woman behind the front desk asked without looking up, still filing the paperwork from the last guest. Shane's heart dropped to his groin. He couldn't see her face as she bent down to pick up a paperclip, but he would know that voice anywhere. The voice he'd heard so many times, in so many different ways. The voice that could drop him to his knees like no other on earth.

Before Shane could answer, a large man carrying a stack of linens walked up to the counter. "Ms. Cooke, where would you like us to set up the tables for tonight's mixer?" he asked, peeking around the side of the stack. "I'm sorry to interrupt, sir —" The stout man stopped in his tracks as soon as he caught a glimpse of Shane and rested the linens on the counter. "Well, look who it is! Shane Knox!"

The woman behind the counter shot her head up at the same time her clipboard dropped with a thud. There Shane was, face-to-face, with the one he'd let slip away so many years ago. Staring him square in the eye, was none other than Avery Cooke.

She looked even more beautiful than he'd remembered, and man, it stung. A lump in his throat threatened to choke him if he didn't find something to say. Her eyes narrowed, and her brows pinched together as she studied him. He couldn't help but remember how sexy she was when she'd get mad, and how her full lips would disappear into a thin line when she was about to give him a piece of her mind. That all too familiar look was now spread across her face, yet he couldn't break the gaze. Her emerald green eyes still mesmerized him; even though he hadn't seen those eyes in nearly nine years, he found a sense of comfort in their familiarity.

"You can set up on the terrace," Avery responded to the man with the linens without breaking her stare with Shane. She knew he'd be coming to town for her brother's wedding—he was the best man after all—but her plan had been to avoid him at all costs. Trapped behind the front desk, she couldn't walk away. There was already a line of other guests forming behind Shane, waiting to check in. No matter how many times she'd run this inevitable moment over in her mind—the moment she'd come face-to-face with *him*—nothing had prepared her for this.

"The name's Knox," Shane said with a grin.

"Yes, Mr. Knox." She played along, finally breaking away to type his name into the computer. She was far too busy to deal with the fact that her first true love was standing before her. A man she hadn't seen in years, the one who'd filled her heart with empty promises before he'd left town and never looked back. "We have you in the Sycamore cabin, one of our best. I'll need an ID and a credit card to get you checked in."

"An ID? Really, Ave?" he asked in a playful tone, which Avery ignored. In this moment, all she wanted to do was get him checked in and out of her sight. And what a sight he was. There was something grown and mature about him, different than the teenage boy he'd once been. Sure, he was always a looker, one of the most popular boys in school, but now his features seemed more defined. His jaw was chiseled beneath his five-o'clock shadow, his upper body visibly cut underneath his snug black T-shirt. A warmth rippled through her body. She had to get him checked in and away from her counter.

Shane pulled his wallet out of his back pocket and handed over the card and ID, his eyes still locked on Avery. "I didn't expect to see you working here."

Avery keyed in the information as fast as she could. She caught a glimpse of his address, and it twisted at her gut: Malibu, California. What was his life like on the other side of the country? It seemed odd that Shane lived on another coast. She dismissed the thought, unwilling to entertain it. For now, she resolved to ignore any small talk and get him out of her line as quickly as possible.

"Well, you know my family owns the resort." She turned and fetched a key from the cabinet behind her and set it on the counter in front of him. "The Sycamore cabin is down by the shore. Just follow the path down the hill, and turn left at the

Beach Cafe. It's the one on the end, set back in the woods. Would you like a map?"

"I remember where the cabins are, Avery." This time he matched her tone, and just like that they were back to their old ways. Their relationship had always been intense; they loved hard and fought even harder. But man, how they'd always loved to make up.

"I'm surprised you remember anything about Arbor Shores at all." She couldn't help herself. The comment had slipped out before she could stop it, but now she was going to regain her composure. She refused to let Shane get to her. "Enjoy your stay at Arbor Shores Resort, Mr. Knox." The key still sat on the counter between them, so Avery nudged it forward, avoiding any chance of their hands making contact. "Next in line?" She craned her neck to call out to the family of four waiting behind him, and just like that, Shane Knox had been dismissed.

"He's arrived? How does he look?" Rylee asked with a light in her eyes as they rearranged the tables on the terrace for the evening event.

"That's beside the point."

"That means he must've looked pretty darn good," Rylee pressed.

"He looks the same as he does online and in the magazines."

"Ah-ha! I knew it. That means you've stalked him online!"

Busted. What could she say? Rylee knew her all too well. Avery didn't want to admit that she had, from time to time, wondered what Shane was up to and who he was dating. Or that she'd not only followed his music career, but she had read every magazine article when he'd married that actress, Naomi Wilde. She'd continued to read even more when Naomi was caught cheating with her co-star on set. Avery had even indulged in the messy divorce that fed the tabloids with juicy Hollywood gossip, and watched as Shane had his heart broken the way he'd broken hers so many years ago.

"Regardless of how he looks, let's be clear; I don't have any interest in him."

"Well, unfortunately for you, he's the best man in your brother's wedding," Rylee reminded her as she set her end of the table down to wipe her palms on her shorts before picking it back up again. "And you're not only in the wedding party, but you're pretty much coordinating most of the wedding festivities at the resort. It's inevitable. You're going to have to see him."

"Ugh, don't remind me."

"This weekend's camping trip should be interesting." Rylee wiggled her eyebrows and smiled.

Dax and Leila had many out-of-town friends in the wedding party, so they decided to host a joint overnight trip instead of having separate bachelor and bachelorette parties. The entire wedding party was scheduled to canoe and camp tomorrow and then be back in time for the rehearsal dinner on Friday.

"I'm not going," Avery declared. She'd made her decision the moment she'd locked eyes with Shane at the front desk.

"Not going where?" Dax asked, walking up behind them with Shane by his side.

Avery wished she'd had time to think before Dax found out. "Uh, I'm not going on the camping trip, Dax." She smoothed the wrinkles from a tablecloth, ignoring Shane altogether. "We're too shorthanded, and I'm needed here."

"No way you're backing out, sis. You're the maid of honor. Leila will be hurt if you don't come." He and Shane moved to opposite ends of a table that was left in the middle of the terrace. "This place will be fine without you for one day. I'll talk to Mom and make sure she's covered. Now, where do you want this table?"

"By the fountain." Avery pointed. She couldn't help but notice the definition in Shane's arms as he lifted the table. Or the way his shirt clung to his defined back. Or the way he looked in those jeans.

"Like what you see?" Rylee whispered with a giggle.

Was Avery's staring that obvious? "Shush, Rylee. Don't you have to get to work?"

"Shoot." Rylee glanced at her watch. "I'd love to stay and see how this plays out." She gave Avery a quick peck on the cheek and turned to head toward the lodge as she called out to the boys, "Bye, guys. Good to see you back home, Shane."

"Good to be back," he said, looking straight at Avery. They locked eyes for a moment before she quickly forced herself to look away.

Her attention turned to Leila when she came bolting down the walkway, determination in her step. "Hi, Ave," Leila greeted her future sister-in-law with a smile but made a beeline straight for her groom. "Dax, I need you to come with me. There's been a change in plans with the menu, something about how they can't get the scallops delivered? We need to test some other options. Chef is plating up some samples for us now."

"Yes, dear." Dax smiled and planted a kiss on his bride's lips. Leila wasn't by any means a bridezilla, but as the wedding drew closer and closer, all the details had her acting a little frantic. Leila was already extremely organized and strong-willed by nature, and Dax couldn't be any more opposite. Dax was more of a free spirit; very little affected his laid-back demeanor. Avery loved watching the dynamic between the two of them. They were yin and yang, salt and pepper, but they balanced each other perfectly. They had been friends since high school, but their friendship blossomed into a relationship after Dax returned home from college a few years ago. They had a deep respect for one another, and the kind of love most women longed for.

As they broke apart, Leila noticed Shane. "Oh, my!" she squealed as she ran over and threw her arms around him. "You made it! We're so glad you're here!"

"Hey, Lei Lei." Shane returned the hug. "I wouldn't miss it for the world."

"Gosh, how long has it been? Eight, nine years?" she asked.

"Nine," Avery chimed in from the table she was setting. Again, the words slipped past her lips without warning. All three of them turned and looked at her, and an awkward silence formed between the group. Avery ignored their collective stares, too embarrassed to look up from the glass she was polishing.

"Well," Leila said, breaking the silence, "I know you two have a lot of catching up to do, and Chef is probably ready for us." She pulled Dax by the hand, leaving Shane and Avery alone on the terrace.

Avery took a deep breath and held it, knowing what was about to come next. A moment she hadn't planned for.

A moment alone with Shane.

CHAPTER 3

*F*inally, Shane was alone with Avery. He'd been hoping for a moment like this since he'd learned he was coming back to Arbor Shores. He had so many things he'd wanted to say for so long, and even more feelings he hadn't realized were buried inside of him. But seeing her brought it all to the surface. It was obvious she was still upset with him, even after all these years, and he needed to make things right before the two of them single-handedly ruined Dax and Leila's wedding.

Avery had turned her back to him and was arranging centerpieces on the tables, ignoring him altogether. Shane didn't mind, because it was giving him a moment to check her out. He hadn't seen her in years, but the attraction between them had always been intense. Feelings like that don't just disappear. He had to admit, the thin teenage girl she once was had morphed into a beautiful woman, and she'd filled out in all the right places. His heart sped up as he searched for a reason to approach her.

As if she could feel his eyes on her, she swung around and marched right up to him, stopping close enough that he could smell her intoxicating scent. Vanilla. Just as sweet as he remembered. "Listen, it's Dax and Leila's wedding, and I'm not going to let anything ruin their weekend." She cocked one hand on her hip.

"I'm not here to ruin anyone's weekend, Ave," Shane responded.

"Please don't call me that. Only those close to me call me Ave."

"Okay, Av-er-y." He made sure to enunciate every syllable of her name, trying to get under her skin. "Can't we just—"

"No, we can't just *anything*," she cut him off before he could finish his sentence. "Let's just keep our distance, okay? You don't talk to me and I won't talk to you."

Now he was growing annoyed. They had dated nearly a decade ago. How was she still upset about things that had happened when they were kids? He knew it would be awkward to see her again after all these years, and he'd spent the past couple of months wondering just how she'd react to his return. Part of him suspected she might be a little bitter, but mostly he hoped she'd be happy he'd come home. So far, it wasn't looking like that was the case.

Avery turned on her heel to leave, but Shane reached out and grabbed her hand, stopping her in her tracks. It was a move that happened so quickly he'd even surprised himself with it. Her delicate hand still fit inside his perfectly, and it felt so natural there. The feeling of her hand in his shot tingles straight up his arm.

"Let go of me," she warned through thin lips. She twisted her hand free, placing it back on her hip.

"Obviously, there's some unfinished business between us. Can't we just talk and clear the air? It will make this weekend more enjoyable for everyone."

"Unfinished business?" Her voice shot up an octave, and the couple who had come out to the terrace to snap a sunset photo quickly moved back inside. They were alone now, high atop the hill, just as the sky was turning shades of magenta and orange. To anyone else, this would have been a romantic setting. "You left town, and you never looked back. You made promises you didn't keep. You never even called, not even when my father died, so I'm sorry if my concern is not in how enjoyable *your* weekend is."

"I know, Ave, but if you could just let me explain myself." His jaw clenched. Why was she painting him out to be the bad guy? He knew the way he'd left may not have been right, but he'd had his reasons. Reasons that stretched far beyond getting too serious with Avery too fast, or his dreams of making it in the music business. Reasons that kept him away from Arbor Shores for far longer than he should have been. Reasons he needed to explain to make her understand.

"Listen, Shane." She stepped closer, closing the space between them. She stood so close, their chests were almost touching. Seeing her up close sent electricity through Shane's entire body. "It's all in the past now, and that's where I'd like to keep it. Let's just stay out of each other's way this weekend for the sake of Dax and Leila."

"Fine, if that's the way you want it."

"Yes, that's the way I want it," she said, but he could swear he heard her voice shake. He watched as she turned and gathered up a stack of linens and headed back inside the resort.

Shane pushed both hands through his hair and kicked at something imaginary on the ground. *Why?* Why did she get under his skin so much? Man, was she stubborn, just as stubborn as he remembered. He couldn't deny, it was that fire in her that attracted him to her in the first place. Shane turned and looked down the hill at the Beach Club below, memories flooding back.

Shane and Dax walked down the dusty path toward the Beach Club, inner tubes resting against their backs as they talked about their summer plans. It felt good to be seniors—finally—and they had every intention of making the most of their last summer in high school.

Down at the Beach Club, they headed straight for the pool, anxious to cool off. Dax's younger sister, Avery, caught Shane's eye. Her baby blue bikini with white polka dots accentuated parts of her figure he'd never knew existed. When had she grown up?

Avery was in the pool, laughing and playing chicken with her friends. She was a grade below him; she must have blossomed when he wasn't paying attention. Her long chestnut hair cascaded down her back, and her tanned body was atop Darren Oberman's shoulders. A wave of jealousy rippled through Shane. Up until that moment, she had always just been his best friend's younger sister. Maybe it was the hormones, maybe it was being seventeen, but it was like he was seeing her for the first time. He dove into the pool and swam over to them while Dax and the rest of the guys went inside the cafe to order food.

"Can I get a turn?" he asked, ready to jump in on the game as they defeated the other team.

"What do you mean can you get a turn?" Avery wriggled down from Darren's shoulders and stood before Shane. "No, you may not!" She made her way to the stairs, abandoning Shane in the pool. Humiliation washed over him. Nobody at Arbor Shores High had ever turned him down. Every girl typically swooned over him, but Avery didn't seem to want anything to do with him. That only intrigued him more.

He watched as she got out of the pool and toweled herself off. Once she was dry, she slipped a white sundress over her head and started off for the beach. The rest of her friends went back to playing chicken, but Shane went after her when nobody was paying attention. He found her walking down the shore.

"Hey, I'm sorry about that back at the pool. I didn't mean to upset you," he said, jogging up beside her.

"Upset me?" She stopped and turned to face him with her hands on her hips. "You asked for a turn with me like I'm some kind of object you can just pass around."

"That's not what I meant." He reached out and took both of her hands in his. She looked down at the gesture but didn't pull away. Shane took that as a good sign. "You all looked like you

were having fun. I just wanted to join in. I didn't mean to offend you."

Her face was softening but no words came out of her mouth. He knew he needed to say more, and he fumbled to find the right words. In that moment, he'd never wanted to kiss a girl so badly as he did Avery. Her lips parted open as if she were going to say something. Her damp swimsuit was soaking through her sundress, and it was doing something to him. Something that made teenage boys say things they normally wouldn't.

"The truth is, I saw you on Darren Oberman's shoulders, and ... I didn't like it."

Her head shot up at his admission and her eyes met his. "Why would you care? You're just my brother's best friend. You and I don't have anything—"

Before she could finish her sentence, he wrapped his arms around her waist, pulling her close. He felt her stiff demeanor soften at his touch, and she tilted her chin up to look at him in the exact moment he leaned in for a kiss—the kiss that seemed to last forever. Slowly, she wrapped her arms around his neck and settled in. He wasn't quite sure what had come over him, but her lips told him she wanted the kiss as badly as he did. There was an immediate connection between them that hadn't existed before. Sure, he'd kissed a few girls before, but it had never felt like this. His lips had found their counterpart, he was certain of it.

From that moment on there was no turning back. Avery Cooke would be the girl to take Shane Knox off the market.

Shane scrubbed his face with his hand and turned his focus away from the Beach Club, trying to erase the memory from his mind—the memory of the kiss that had started the best summer of his life.

Avery headed straight for the employee bathroom and locked the door. She slumped against the back of the door and slid to the ground. Why was she letting him get to her? She was over Shane Knox. Sure, she'd spent years crying over him, but that had stopped long ago. She'd even had a serious boyfriend in her early twenties, Tim Thompson, that she'd dated for three years and almost married. True, she'd broken it off with him once she began running the hotel, but that was only because she needed to focus on her career, wasn't it? Doubt niggled at her brain. It wasn't just career related. Something had definitely been missing in their relationship. But that something hadn't had anything to do with Shane.

So why was she so upset to see Shane after all this time? *Was she overacting?* Now she was beginning to feel foolish for the way she'd treated him. She didn't want him to think she still carried resentment. It was just that having him here at the resort, where they had so much history together, was bringing up emotions she thought she'd buried deep. Memories of sneaking into the vacant cabins to make out, memories of weekend bonfires down by the lake, memories of that night when they'd taken a blanket out to hole seven of the golf course, with only the stars above bearing witness.

She rose to her feet and splashed some water on her face and dabbed any trace of mascara from under her eyes. She had to pull it together for Dax and Leila. She refused to act like this every time she ran into Shane over the next several days. Besides, it was making her look as if she still cared for him, and she didn't want to give anyone that impression. There was no reason to be so angry.

Avery stared at her reflection and steeled her nerves. Shane would never know he still got to her. She wouldn't let him think she had even an ounce of feelings for him left inside. If she had to pretend, she'd pretend.

Because Shane could never know she'd never truly gotten over him.

～

Avery pushed out of the bathroom and paused, backing into the doorway when she saw a man leaving her mother's office. The man disappeared around the corner before Avery could make out who he was.

Her mother turned. "There you are, dear." She smiled warmly at Avery. "Oh my, you don't look so good. Is everything okay?" she asked, concern in her eyes.

"I'm fine," Avery said. "I just ate something that didn't agree with me." She looked past her mother, in the direction the man had gone. "Was that Hunter Knox you were just talking to? Why is he here?"

"Oh, just a business idea he wanted to run past me." Meredith looked down and fiddled with the dial on her watch. "Why don't you go on home now and get some rest? I'll watch the front desk for the rest of the evening."

"A business idea?" Avery wasn't letting her mother change the subject on this one. She knew Hunter was into commercial real estate development, and when he wanted something, family-owned businesses were no match for his power and money. Especially businesses that weren't doing well, like the resort. A wave of panic rushed through her system. "What kind of idea would Hunter have for Arbor Shores Resort?"

"Nothing that I'm going to entertain so don't worry yourself with it. You just go on home and take care of yourself."

Avery was sure there was more to this conversation, but she didn't have the energy to pry it out of her mother. They'd had plenty of conversations about how they needed to do something drastic to increase sales at the resort. She didn't want to bring it up now. Not when they had the wedding to focus on. "I think I'll take you up on that. The terrace is all set up for tonight," she said as she headed toward the office to grab her purse. She was anxious to get away from the resort and any chance of another run-in with Shane.

"Oh, and Avery?" her mother called after her. "I talked to your brother. You're going on the camping trip tomorrow, so rest up. You've been working far too hard around here, and you need to enjoy yourself for a change. I have everything covered on this end."

Great. There was no getting out of it now. Still, she knew her mother's words were true. She *had* been working far too much lately. She couldn't even remember the last time she'd taken a trip with friends. But taking a day off was hard. Despite how hard Avery had thrown herself into her work, things at the resort still weren't great. A few more months without improvement, and the Cookes would likely lose the resort. With summer homes being converted into vacation rentals, new rental options were popping up all over Arbor Shores, and fewer and fewer families were staying at the resort each summer. They'd had to lay off several employees to cut expenses, which meant Avery and her mother had to work twice as hard. Dax was the golf pro at the resort, so that kept him busy with lessons most days, which meant the bulk of the responsibilities fell on Avery and Meredith. Plus, with Dax's upcoming wedding, they hadn't wanted to worry him with anything that might take away from his special day. Dax was completely in the dark regarding the state of the resort's financials. He didn't know that they were on track to have their worst summer yet, and that the wedding was causing added debt that was putting them in the red.

Avery just smiled at her mother and turned back toward the office. With Mom taking Dax's side, there was no way to get out of the camping trip. Could she handle being trapped for an entire day and night with Shane?

She *did* need to get away from the resort. It was the only way she might possibly clear her head. She grabbed her things and headed straight for the door. She knew just the place.

CHAPTER 4

"Hey there, Avery," Big John called out from behind the bar at Ripples. Each barstool was filled, some with faces she recognized, the rest she assumed by tourists. Ripples always attracted a crowd. It was known for keeping local beers on tap, and offering farm-to-table dishes grown by local farmers just inland from Arbor Shores. It was something Avery had always wanted to implement at the resort but hadn't gotten around to yet.

"Hi, John. Where's Rylee's section today?"

"On the patio. Good luck finding a seat though."

As luck would have it, Avery found Rylee clearing a two top on the corner of the deck. This was ideal because it had the perfect lake view and a clear shot of the band, but still gave her some privacy in the corner, which Avery desperately needed.

"Girl, I know you're making money out here today. This place is packed," Avery said, walking up behind her friend.

Rylee whipped around at the sound of Avery's voice. "Hey! What are you doing here? You're never out of work this early." It was true. Avery usually got to work at the crack of dawn and stayed most evenings until the last event was over, which sometimes meant nine or ten at night. To be out this early, the time the rest of America was heading home from work, was unheard of. She didn't have much to go home to other than her cat, Tipper, and today was the perfect summer day—high seventies and full sunshine. She planned to have something to eat, and perhaps take a walk on the beach. She hadn't had much beach time since summer broke, and her creamy skin could use some sun.

"I was on my way home, and thought I'd stop for a quick bite. With all the wedding plans and the chamber event tonight, I forgot to eat today. Is this seat open?"

"For you? Always." Rylee shot up an eyebrow as she surveyed her friend's face. "You always flee to the beach when you need to clear your head. You okay?"

"Can't a girl just stop to see her best friend?"

"Hmm, are you sure there isn't something else that brought you here?"

"What are you talking about? I'll take a glass of iced tea and the cherry chicken salad, please." She didn't need a menu. That was her go-to meal whenever she got a chance to stop by Ripples.

"Got it." Rylee gave the table one final wipe and nodded in the direction of the beach. "I just thought maybe you'd come to meet Shane."

Avery followed Rylee's gaze to find Shane standing by the shore, swarmed by people waiting to talk with him and get photos. He was kneeling down, posing with a little boy while the boy's mother snapped pictures.

"What's he doing here?" Avery asked, taking a moment to watch the way Shane ruffled the boy's hair and held him on his knee for the pictures.

"I don't know but he's been out there for close to thirty minutes. People won't leave him alone. I can't imagine what that must be like."

"Miss, can we get some menus over here?" a man called out from two tables over, and Rylee headed in their direction, leaving Avery alone with her thoughts. And a clear view of Shane.

She watched as he obliged, smiling for photos as everyone from young teens to forty-something moms took turns posing with him. She admired his patience; it was making her tired just watching. But he didn't show any sign of annoyance. If he was bothered by the attention, he sure hid it well. As the crowd began to clear, he slowly made his way to the patio stairs when another crowd from inside the restaurant rushed out and approached him for another round of photos.

Just as Rylee delivered Avery's iced tea and some bread, the band came back from break and began to fill the stage set up on the patio. "Hey, folks," the singer said into the microphone. "Do you see what I see? If it isn't Arbor Shores' one and only, Shane Knox in the house!"

The entire deck erupted with applause. Ladies squealed and men whistled, giving Shane a warm welcome. All the attention showered on her ex-boyfriend made Avery lose what little appetite she'd mustered up.

Shane gave a wave over his head to the crowd and flashed a smile in the direction of his fans, nodding to the singer for acknowledging him.

"I wonder if we could get Shane up here to sing a song for us," the singer announced, causing the crowd to erupt even louder. Even families having dinner stopped to watch, and kids stood on their chairs to catch a glimpse of Shane.

"Ah, not today. These folks came out to see you."

But the singer wasn't giving up. "Come on now, Shane. We'd be honored to share the stage with you. Just one song?"

Someone in the crowd began clapping and chanting his name, and before long the entire patio was beckoning him in unison, "Shane, Shane, Shane, Shane ..."

Avery watched in disbelief. This was his everyday life? She'd known he was famous, but she'd never really thought about what that actually meant.

Shane finally gave in and headed onto the stage. "All right, just one song won't hurt," he announced into the microphone, and the crowd erupted once again.

One of the band members handed Shane a guitar. He strummed a few chords as he looked out over the crowd. It wasn't long before his eyes found Avery's. A lump formed in her throat. She held his gaze for a moment until she finally forced herself to look away.

"What would you like to play for them?" the bass player called out to Shane.

"I know just the song," Avery heard him say. She looked out over the beach and studied the waves lapping the shore. Could she somehow duck out? She was in the far corner of the patio, farthest from the stairs; she'd have to walk right past the stage to leave.

Shane turned and talked to the bass player, then the drummer, then took his place back center stage at the microphone. The music started, and so did Shane's lyrics.

Chills pricked at the back of Avery's neck as he sang. Man, he had a great voice. He sounded even better live than on the radio. She recognized the lyrics from one of his first hit ballads, *Back to You*, one of the first that ever topped the charts and put his band on the map. She knew every word of the song by heart. She'd listened to it over and over and cried herself to sleep a thousand times.

She couldn't take her eyes off him as he sang. She studied his face when he closed his eyes to hit the deep notes, and she watched the way he stopped playing the guitar and grasped the microphone tightly when he sang the final words.

No matter where I go, no matter what I do ...
There will never be another love so true.
Someday, girl, I'll come back to you ...
You ... I'll come back to you ...

Shane opened his eyes and looked straight at Avery as he sang that last line. As he strummed his final chord on the guitar, she finally forced herself to break away. Where was her salad, anyway? She was beginning to feel uncomfortable, and by the looks she was receiving from everyone around her, the crowd had decided that Shane had been singing to her.

Was it the words, or the sight of Shane, or the combination of both that was stirring emotion in her? She had to get out of there, and fast.

Shane high-fived each member of the band and handed the guitar back to the lead singer as the crowd stood and cheered. It wasn't every day that Ripples had a famous rock star on stage, and it had caused quite a commotion. Avery knew this was her opportunity to get out of there. She suspected he was trying to make his way to her table, but he was swarmed by a sea of fans who'd gotten up from their seats to greet him as he exited the stage.

"Wow, that was clearly for you. You know that, right?" Rylee returned to top off Avery's tea and deliver her salad.

"I'll take my check," Avery told her friend as she gathered her things.

"Right now? You haven't eaten yet."

"Right now."

"Go, I've got this one." Rylee winked at Avery, offering her a knowing smile.

"You sure?"

"Of course. Love ya." Rylee left just before Shane reached the table.

"This seat taken?" he asked, pulling out the chair across from Avery.

"The table is yours. I was just leaving." Avery tried to swallow the emotion that had risen to the surface.

"You haven't even eaten your food. Let's catch up." He sank into the seat across from her. All eyes were on them, but at least people were returning to their seats, staring from a more polite distance.

"I have to go." She stood and grabbed her purse hanging on the back of her chair. *Stay strong, Avery. Just walk away.*

"Avery, please," he pleaded. There was a sincerity in his voice that almost made her break.

"Actually, I have somewhere to be." That couldn't be further from the truth. She fetched a ten-dollar bill from her wallet and put the saltshaker over it. "Please see to it that Rylee gets that."

Avery somehow managed to walk away, legs shaking, but still, she was upright so that had to count for something. She could feel what must've been a thousand eyes on her as she exited the patio, leaving Shane alone at the table. She couldn't get out of there fast enough. So much for her walk on the beach. She'd be lucky if her legs carried her to her car.

She just needed to get home where she could finally cry the tears that had been building up inside of her all day.

Shane was left alone at the table with nothing but his bruised ego and the salad sitting across from him. He could feel everyone's eyes on him and it made his skin itch. He was ready to get out of there.

He glanced at his watch. Quarter to six. He was due at the Knox estate for dinner in fifteen minutes, something he'd been dreading since his arrival. News traveled fast in this small town, and when Carter Knox got word that his estranged son had returned to Arbor Shores, Shane got a call from his stepmother, Valerie, to arrange the dinner.

Shane didn't care for his father or Valerie. He still had a good relationship with his mother, but she lived in Florida, far from the sting of the nasty divorce battle that had ensued for nearly two years once she'd discovered Carter had been having a decade-long affair with his executive assistant. Shane blamed his father and Valerie for the demise of the family, and the pain and humiliation they'd caused his mother. He hadn't spoken to either one of them since he'd left nine years ago. To say this dinner was going to be awkward was an understatement.

"Shane, can I get you something?" Rylee appeared with a rag in hand, scooping up Avery's salad and wiping the table. "A cold beer maybe?"

"Nah, thanks anyway. I have to get out of here." He got up and grabbed his aviators that were hanging from his shirt and put them on. "Can I just ask you something?"

"Go for it. As long as it's quick. I'm slammed out here today." Rylee paused to wait for his question.

"Why won't she talk to me? I mean, I understand she's upset about the way things ended. But that was so long ago. Why does she still hate me?"

"Oh, Shane. That's not hate." Rylee tossed the towel over her shoulder and gave his arm a sympathetic squeeze. "Hate doesn't have anything to do with it." She gave him a wink and headed to greet a new table.

CHAPTER 5

*S*hane drove fast down Pine Ridge Way, taking the curves like a racecar driver. He'd always loved driving down this road; it was the going home part that he'd never cared for. He flipped on his left blinker, ready to pull into Lakeview Estates, a gated community just south of town where the wealthiest of Arbor Shores resided. The community was set across from the yacht club and marina where the residents docked their boats. There was only one road in, and it snaked up a large hill with sprawling estates spread acres apart from one another. At the top of the hill sat the Knox residence, which overlooked all of Arbor Shores below and boasted the most breathtaking view of Lake Michigan you could find.

As he approached the guard shack, a middle-aged man with peppered hair came out and held up his hand, motioning for Shane to stop.

"May I help you?" the man asked.

"Knox estate."

The man looked him over. "Your name?"

Shane was growing annoyed. It wasn't often that people didn't recognize him. "Shane Knox."

"ID," the man demanded, not moving from beside the vehicle.

"You've got to be kidding. Where's Ben?" Shane peered around the man to see if anyone else was in the guard shack. Ben had manned the gate for as long as Shane could remember.

"I'll need some ID. All guests must be announced and approved."

Shane fetched his ID from his wallet and handed it over with an audible sigh. The man disappeared into the shack for what seemed like an eternity.

"Clear." The man finally returned and handed Shane's ID back, with no apology for the hassle. "Follow this road all the way to the end. The Knox estate is at the top of the hill."

Shane snatched his ID back, maybe a little too aggressively. How did this man not recognize him? He put the car in drive and headed through the gate. As annoyed as he was at the guard, he was thankful for the delay. Any minute he could delay this dinner was fine with him.

The road wound around sprawling acres with homes set back on manicured lawns, until it reached the top of the hill, and there, towering high above Arbor Shores, sat his childhood home. The Knox estate was the largest single-family residence in the region, with rolling greens for the front lawn, and a backdrop of evergreens behind it. When Shane was a young boy, he had thought those trees reached all the way to the sky. The massive home was chalet-style and could be seen all the way from town. From there, it looked more like a ski resort than a home.

He put his car in park and got out just as Valerie made her way down the front walk to greet him. "Shane, welcome. So nice to see you here. It's been far too long." She leaned in for a light hug, which took Shane by surprise. He had never once hugged her, not even close. He noticed she didn't seem as young and scandalous as he remembered. She had to be at least forty-five now, although not even a hint of age lines showed around her eyes. She was still strikingly beautiful with long, silky black hair and ice-blue eyes. Her looks were obviously well-maintained. Shane knew the look of Botox and fillers well. She looked just like every other gold digger he'd run across in LA.

"Yes, it has been a bit." He stepped back to create space between them. "Dad around?"

"Oh, yes, he's inside pacing a hole in the floor. You know how he feels about punctuality." She gave him a pointed look as she tapped a shiny red nail on her diamond encrusted watch. *Punctuality?* It was only seven past the hour. It's not his fault they hadn't announced him to the guard as a visitor.

Shane ignored her comment and followed her up a long, flower-lined path that led from the driveway to the front door. The welcoming scent of honeysuckle filled the air. They were high atop the lake and the views of blue freshwater stretched so far it was hard to tell where the water ended and the sky began. The air felt a few degrees cooler up here than it had in town. He'd forgotten about this view. Or maybe he'd just never appreciated it before.

Valerie led Shane through the foyer and straight to the library where Carter was standing with his back to the door, arms crossed and gazing out the window. Shane's stomach twisted into a knot at the sight of his father. The smell of expensive leather and cigars lingered in the air, transporting him to unhappier times. Growing up, his father had always called each of the Knox boys into the library one by one when they were in trouble. As the eldest of the four boys, Shane usually got the worst of it. Just being in this room made his stomach turn.

"Carter, dear, Shane has arrived," Valerie announced. "I'll leave you two to catch up. Dinner's in ten minutes."

"Shane." Carter Knox barely acknowledged his son as he turned around, not looking him in the eye more than a brief second before taking his place behind the desk.

"Dad." Shane mirrored his tone. He was still bitter, and not just about the divorce, or that his father had never supported his music career. Shane carried around too much baggage, all related to the way his father treated him. He wasn't willing to let it all go just because he was back in town for the weekend.

"Sit," Carter demanded, motioning toward the seat across from him. "I hear you're back in town for Dax Cooke's wedding."

Shane took a seat in one of the two leather armchairs situated across from the desk. Still the same chairs he remembered all too well, although this one felt a bit smaller than he remembered.

"He and Leila are getting married on Saturday at Arbor Shores Resort. Dax asked me to stand up in his wedding. I wouldn't miss it," Shane said.

"So that's what it takes to bring you back home after all these years? A wedding?"

Here we go. "I didn't have a reason to come back before."

"Your family isn't reason enough?" Carter leaned forward and peered over his glasses.

"Listen, I don't really want to get into all of this." Shane scrubbed his hand over his face and sat up straight. "I was hoping we'd be able to set our issues aside for one evening."

"And what issues are those, Shane?" Carter was not going to let up, and Shane was growing more annoyed by the second. "I didn't know we had any issues. All I know is that you left Arbor Shores nine years ago, and nobody in this town has seen you since. You've been too busy becoming some drifter trying to play music to—"

"A drifter trying to play music?" Shane rose to his feet, prepared to give his father a piece of his mind. He couldn't believe it. He'd finally made it. His band was one of the most famous of their time, and his father still wouldn't acknowledge his success?

Words pulsed inside Shane, but he couldn't say any of them. There was something about his father that still intimidated him, something that stopped him from saying what he really wanted to say. "Coming here was a mistake."

"Sit down, Shane," his father demanded in a steady tone,

making Shane feel foolish for getting worked up. How did his father still manage to make him feel so small? Shane sank back in his chair and stared his father down, waiting for his next passive-aggressive remark.

"Chef Louis has prepared a nice dinner, and Hunter will be joining us. Surely we can enjoy *one* meal as a family."

A family? This was not a family. Shane's band was his family. His fans were his family. As far as Shane was concerned, his father had lost the right to call this a family when he'd decided to step out on his mother and bring a new woman into their home. This would never be a family to Shane. It took everything he had to keep years' worth of anger from slipping past his lips.

The large mahogany library doors cracked open, and Valerie poked her head in. "Hunter just pulled in. Let's move this to the dining room, shall we?"

Shane had never been so happy to see Valerie. One more second and surely he would've given his father a piece of his music-chasing mind.

"Well, well, if it isn't our long-lost rock star." Hunter entered the dining room, leaning in to kiss Valerie on the cheek. The sight of Hunter's affection and approval of her in their mother's home warmed Shane's blood.

Shane ignored his brother's snarky remark. Truth is, he'd never been too close to Hunter. They were polar opposites. Of the four Knox brothers, Shane was the oldest and Hunter was the youngest, with four years between them. The brothers didn't even share one common interest. Hunter was on track to become the youngest billionaire Michigan had ever known. Once he took over the family business, that is. As the baby of the family, Hunter was always favored, and in Shane's opinion, he was the do-good boy who lived his life for Carter's approval. It nauseated Shane beyond words. Their other two brothers were twins, and they both left Arbor Shores separately after they graduated high school a year after Shane. Ethan was recruited to play college football for the University of Michigan and then went on to go pro when he was drafted to the NFL. Chase, the other twin, was the real drifter of the family. Shane didn't know where he was; they had lost touch long ago.

"Aren't you going to say hello to your brother, Shane?" His father raised an eyebrow in his direction as he took his spot at the head of the table.

"If it isn't Mr. Businessman himself," Shane mocked. Two could play this game.

"Boys, please sit. Jeffrey is ready to serve dinner," Valerie interjected, breaking up the banter. The family butler hovered in the doorway with a large bowl in each hand, waiting for everyone to take their seats.

"Jeffrey!" Shane was happier to see the family butler than anyone else in the room. "Good to see you're still here, my man."

"Shane, nice to see you come home, boy!" Jeffrey put down the salads and made his way around the table, filling each water goblet. "I've been following your music career all these years. You've really made something special of yourself." He flashed a proud smile in Shane's direction. Jeffrey had been more of a father figure to Shane than Carter ever had. It was Jeffrey that had shown Shane how to throw a baseball, taught him how to fish, had the birds and the bees talk that fathers are supposed to have with their sons. Carter had never been around for those moments. Always too busy out chasing the mighty dollar. Another thing Shane still held resentment over.

Valerie cleared her throat, and Jeffrey disappeared out the door without another word.

"Shane, I was sorry to read about you and Naomi," Valerie said. "It must be hard dating actresses with the way they are always on location. That distance would surely put a damper on any relationship."

"We weren't dating, we were married." Shane closed his fist around his fork. "And distance or not, we took vows. Some people hold those vows sacred." His father's glare bore into him, and he almost regretted his words as fast as he'd said them. Nah, he meant it. Shane was bitter. He was bitter at Naomi, and he was bitter at his father and Valerie.

"I saw Avery Cooke today. Have you seen her yet?" Shane's head shot in Hunter's direction. "She's looking pretty good."

"Where did you see Avery?"

"Didn't Dad tell you? I'm acquiring Arbor Shores Resort. I was there this afternoon finalizing the terms with Meredith Cooke."

"Acquiring the resort?" Shane stared at his brother in shock. The resort had been in the Cooke family for over fifty years. Passed down through the family from Avery's grandfather. Families had been vacationing there since the sixties. It was one of the most iconic vacation destinations in the region.

"Why do you sound surprised?" Hunter challenged.

"You just don't strike me as someone who would want to own a family-style resort, that's all."

"I don't, and I won't." Hunter paused to take a sip of his wine.

"What are your plans for it?" Shane asked, trying to play it cool.

"That's the best piece of commercial property in Arbor Shores. The resort is a tear down." Carter chimed in. "Hunter's been looking for a nice piece of waterfront land to develop into luxury condos. Arbor Shores Resort will be perfect, once we demolish and rebuild."

"Demolish and rebuild? What's wrong with keeping it as is?" Shane tossed down his salad fork, making a clanging noise against the other utensils and causing Valerie to flinch. "People love that resort. The cabins and the Beach Club are what draw so many tourists to this area every summer."

"So now you're a real estate expert?" Hunter jabbed. "Why don't you stick to playing music and leave business to us."

Shane pushed his chair back, ready to get up. He'd suddenly lost his appetite and was ready to remove himself from this dinner once and for all.

"The Cooke's are in trouble, Shane," Valerie began. "That place hasn't been profitable since Sal Cooke passed away. Families rent summer homes and condos now. Fewer and fewer families are visiting the resort."

"Things have changed since you left. But we wouldn't expect you to know anything about that," his father added.

Shane rose to his feet. "Valerie, thank you for the invitation." He nodded in his stepmother's direction. "Dad, Hunter." Shane had a million things running through his mind that he wanted to say to each of them, but he knew better than to waste the energy. Nothing he could ever say would make a difference.

"Shane, dear ..." Valerie stood as he headed for the door.

"Let him go," he heard his father tell her. And that's exactly what Shane did. Straight out the door of Knox residence for what he knew in his heart would be the last time.

CHAPTER 6

*A*very poured herself a mug of coffee and felt something soft rub against her leg.

"You hungry, boy?" Like clockwork, Tipper was waiting for his morning meal. She opened the pantry and fetched a can of cat food, peeling off the tin lid and dumping the contents into his bowl. She grabbed her coffee and headed out back to the deck, her favorite part of her home. Drinking her coffee on the deck was something she tried to do every morning that time allowed.

Her small two-bedroom home was just a few miles outside of town. Set back in the woods, it gave her just the privacy she longed for. She'd always loved nature, and her backyard was surrounded with mature trees that backed up to state land that would never be developed. She loved sitting out there in the morning, watching the birds, feeling the crisp air, and taking in the sounds and smells of the forest that surrounded her. She couldn't see her neighbors, and that was just how she liked it. The scent of sweet evergreen awakened her senses—just what she needed after the terrible sleep she'd gotten the night before.

Avery's cell phone buzzed on the patio table, startling her. She wasn't ready for the outside world just yet. She glanced at the screen. *Dax*.

"Morning," she answered.

"Good, you're up. I was hoping I wasn't going to have to come over there."

"Why wouldn't I be up, Dax? I'm the morning person out of the two of us, remember?" She pulled her feet onto the Adirondack chair and tucked them under her legs, taking a sip of her coffee. "What are *you* doing up at this hour is a better question."

"Just making sure you're ready for the trip. We're meeting at Crystal River in two hours." Avery took the phone from her ear to glance at the time on the screen. Seven o'clock.

"Remind me why we are leaving so early." Avery had planned most of the wedding festivities that were scheduled to take place at the resort, but she didn't know much about this trip, other than it involved canoeing to their overnight campsite, something she would normally love. But knowing Shane would be there, she was dreading it.

"We check in at the river at nine. They'll bus us north with the canoes to the drop-off point. We will spend the day canoeing back to the campsite where everything is already set up for us. Shane and I went there last night and pitched the tents and gathered wood. We're good to go." Her brother sounded excited and she didn't want her dread to put a damper on his day. "It's great to see Shane after all these years, huh, Ave?"

"I have to get in the shower," Avery said, quick to change the subject.

"Nine o'clock. You'd better be there."

"Bye, Dax." She tossed the phone onto the chair next to her and stretched her arms above her head. No doubt, this was going to be one interesting day.

Avery pulled her car into the parking lot of the canoe livery. She could see a crowd of people had already formed outside a bus with a trailer of canoes stacked behind it. She parked, grabbed her overnight bag, and headed toward Leila. She could pick Leila's blonde hair out of a crowd anywhere. Leila had a beauty about her, but it was her dynamic personality and kind heart that really made her shine. She was telling a story to the six people gathered near her, and her infectious laugh echoed through the quiet woods around them.

Avery recognized the crew as Dax and Leila's wedding party. To Leila's right was Aiden and Carley, a couple she and Dax always hung out with. To her left there was Leila's best friend from college, Jen, and her husband Gavin. Across from her stood Cooper and Chelsea, Leila's twin cousins whom Avery suspected she'd invited to be in the wedding party to appease the family, though they did round out a perfectly sized wedding party—three bridesmaids and three groomsmen. Leila had asked Avery to be her maid of honor, probably because Leila was an only child and Avery was the closest thing she had to a sister. Though Avery had wondered more than once if it had something to do with Shane being the best man. He was single, or so she thought. Maybe they needed single Avery to balance him out?

Avery didn't know much about the twins apart from their obviously stunning good looks. Cooper had a clean-cut appearance, his sandy blond hair buzzed short, and his face clean-shaven. Avery guessed him to be a cop or a lawyer. Chelsea, on the other hand, had fiery red hair and a wild look about her. They were both attractive in their own way, but they sure didn't look like twins. They didn't even look like siblings.

"Avery, you made it!" Leila greeted her as she approached the group. Shane turned from the cooler he was filling with ice at the announcement of her name. Her eyes met Shane's for a brief moment, before she quickly looked back to Leila.

"I wouldn't miss it." Not entirely true. If she could've found a way out of the trip without hurting Leila's feelings, she probably wouldn't be there. "Where should I put my bag?"

"Bags go in the front two seats of the bus. The driver will take them to our camp after he drops us at the mouth of the river." Dax walked up from behind his sister and grabbed the bag off her shoulder and headed toward the bus with it.

Leila went back to telling her story. Avery could feel Shane's eyes on her. She had managed not to make eye contact again, but she could see him making his way over in her direction out of the corner of her eye. She looked around. Wasn't there somewhere she could go? Something she could do?

"Morning," Shane said, approaching her. "Beautiful day, huh?"

"Mornings are always beautiful in Arbor Shores," Avery responded, closing her eyes and taking in a deep breath of the forest air.

"So, they have us paired together in a canoe. I hope you're okay with that? I didn't have anything to do with it, just so you know." He held his hands up innocently.

Great. This day was not off to a good start. There was nothing she could do. The only other option was to split up the twins, but the thought of Shane canoeing with Chelsea made her stomach flip.

"I figured as much. Just so long as you don't tip us." A grin slipped past her lips.

Shane and Avery had spent many summer days canoeing down this exact river with their high school friends. On one particular trip, they had gone out on Memorial Day, at the very beginning of summer. The water was still ice cold, and Shane had promised Avery that she wouldn't have to touch the water for the entire trip. About two minutes in, Shane turned to announce to the canoes behind them that there was a bend up ahead in the river, and just as he turned in his seat, the canoe tipped to the left, dumping both of them into the water. They'd spent the rest of the afternoon cold and wet, fighting the whole way down the river. Until that night, when they'd made up by the campfire after everyone else had gone to sleep.

"This time, I'm not going to make any promises." He winked at Avery.

"You'd better promise." She pointed a finger at him with a smile. "It's still early summer and that water is frigid." She caught herself warming up to him, but she wasn't ready to let her guard down just yet. She headed toward the bus to find her brother.

～

The bus ride was bumpy but fun. Dax and Shane reminisced about trips down the river and retold stories from their past. Avery stared out the window to hide her smile, but listening to the two friends tell their tales brought back some great memories. She particularly loved hearing the excitement in her brother's voice again. Dax was always so happy and carefree, something Avery loved about him, but he had lost some of his spirit since their father passed away. Having Shane back in town was bringing out a joy in him Avery had really missed. Maybe this trip wouldn't be so bad after all.

When they finally reached the drop-off point, they all filed off the bus, and the guys immediately went to work untying the canoes from the trailer and lining them up on the shore. The morning sun was getting higher in the sky, and it was already nearly eighty degrees, which meant it was going to be a hot day. It was a bit out of the ordinary for June in Arbor Shores, but was ideal for a day on the water.

Avery watched as Shane grabbed two life preservers and threw them into the canoe along with a small cooler. After everything was settled, he tugged at the back of his shirt and pulled it over his head, exposing his bare chest and six-pack abs. He tossed his shirt into the canoe, opened the cooler, grabbed a water and started chugging it. Avery, along with every other female on shore, stopped what they were doing to watch. Shane was always a looker, but now he had grown up, and his rugged good looks were something you'd see in a magazine. And she had. She remembered seeing him look just like this when the paparazzi had snapped photos of him and Naomi Wilde on the beach in Bali on their honeymoon. He had the same look today: a hint of five-o'clock shadow, intentionally messy hair, tan skin, and abs that went on for days. She recalled how it had stung to see his arms wrapped around Naomi and the smile on his face as he looked longingly into her eyes.

"Whatcha lookin' at?" Leila teased, poking Avery in the ribs.

"Hey, Lei. You ready for a day of fun on the river?"

"Don't change the subject." Leila wasn't going to let this one go. She leaned in and whispered, "You know, he asks Dax about you all the time."

"Huh?" Avery was confused. She didn't know that Dax and Shane had even stayed in contact all that much.

"It's true. He's always asking Dax how you're doing. He tells Dax to say hello for him each time they talk."

That was strange. Dax had never mentioned speaking to Shane until the wedding planning began, and her brother certainly never told her Shane had asked about her.

"Dax has never mentioned anything," Avery admitted.

"I'm sure he's just trying to protect you, like big brothers do."

"Protect me?"

"The way Dax explains it, you were crushed when Shane left to pursue his music career. He said it took you years to get over him. He probably doesn't want to see you get hurt again."

Heat pricked at Avery's cheeks. Years to get over him? A mixture of anger and humiliation swirled inside her at the thought of her brother speaking about her heartache to someone else. Had he told Shane the same thing? She didn't want Shane to think she'd been pining after him all these years, though it had taken a long time for her to stop thinking about him every day.

It wasn't just that he'd broken her heart. She was more upset about all the empty promises he'd made. Nobody else knew about those, about how much he'd truly crushed her hopes for their relationship. Her pride couldn't stand the idea of Shane thinking she still wasn't over him, that she'd been heartbroken all these years. She had to play it cool. She had to show everyone that she was truly over Shane.

"Ready, Ave?" Shane called to her with his hand held out, ready to help her into the canoe.

"Actually, I was thinking I'd canoe with Cooper." She looked over at the twins. "Chelsea, do you want to switch spots with me?"

Chelsea's face lit up like she'd just won the lottery. Avery instantly regretted her words. What had she done? Did she really just put beautiful and wild Chelsea in a canoe with her rock star ex-boyfriend?

Avery let out a sigh. This was going to be one long day on the river.

CHAPTER 7

*S*hane could see Avery up ahead, chatting and laughing
with Cooper in their canoe. He was trying not to get
upset that she was having fun with another guy on the exact river
where they had made so many memories together. Was she interested in Cooper? Seeing Avery being friendly with someone else
made his blood boil, even if they were just talking.

Where was this jealousy coming from anyway? He thought
he'd gotten over Avery long ago. But then again, a day seldom
went by that he didn't think about her at least once. Even on his
wedding day with Naomi, a vision of Avery had flashed through
his mind right before he said *I do.* From time to time, Avery
even showed up in his dreams. He always chalked it up to the
fact that the two of them had never really gotten any closure, not
with the way he had left. This trip back home was the perfect
opportunity for him to finally explain himself and get the closure
they both deserved. It was his chance to tell her the full story—
the truth. Then, hopefully, she would let go of any resentment
she still held for him. If only she'd let down her guard long
enough for him to get her alone. He at least owed that to her. He
may have been young and stupid to leave the way he did, but

this was his chance to make things right. And for whatever reason, right now, that felt more important to him than anything.

It was high noon, and they'd been on the water for a couple of hours. The sun was intense and Avery had taken off her sundress. All the other women were in their swimsuits as well, but Avery was the only one who captured Shane's attention. Even though he was sharing a canoe with what most men would consider a drop-dead knockout, in his eyes, Chelsea didn't have anything on Avery.

Their canoe was behind Avery and Cooper's, offering him the perfect view of the duo. Avery's beauty radiated, and each time she'd tilt her chin up to allow the sun to warm her face, Shane would catch himself becoming fixated on her. Every so often, Cooper would lightly flick his paddle in the water and give her a splash. She'd squeal as the cool water hit her bare back, and they'd both erupt in giggles. Their laughter nipped at him. It should be Shane in that canoe, not Cooper. Was Cooper trying to flirt with her? He couldn't blame him if he was. But watching Avery with Cooper was causing him to grow impatient, and he couldn't wait for this trek down the river to end. Why had she switched canoes at the last minute? Just before that moment, it almost seemed like she was starting to warm up to him, and he'd been looking forward to their time alone in the canoe. He was starting to think he'd never get the opportunity to talk to her privately.

By the time they reached the campsite, Shane's mood had soured. He couldn't watch Avery smiling and having fun with someone else in his place. By now, he was convinced she was actually into Cooper, and it left a hollow feeling in his heart.

Shane couldn't believe his eyes. Avery had to be trying to upset him, he was sure of it. Ever since they had gotten off the river and settled at camp, she had been chatting with Cooper, laughing and fully engrossed in whatever story he was telling.

He felt like a fool obsessing over the two of them, so he resolved to turn the rest of the evening around. Why was he so fixed on his ex, anyway? She didn't belong to him anymore and hadn't for a long time. It was time to give it a rest and find something to take his mind off of the situation. He headed for the cooler to grab a beer and found Chelsea sitting alone at a picnic table, taking a selfie on her phone.

"Want me to take that for you?" he asked, setting his beer down across from her.

"Actually, I'd love it if we could take one together." She rose to her feet and made her way around the picnic table, all smiles. Shane was sure the photo would end up on social media, and then he would have to answer to the tabloids about who the new vivacious redhead was in his life. Still, he had to get Avery's attention one way or another. He remembered her mild jealous streak, and he knew a photo op with Chelsea would get under her skin.

He put his arm around Chelsea's waist and pulled her in for the selfie, smiling from ear to ear as he held the phone out and took the picture. Chelsea nuzzled into his chest as if she were claiming him as her own. Maybe he had taken it too far? Nah, it was only a picture.

He could feel Avery's eyes on them, yet the rest of the crew seemed oblivious to what was happening. The guys were gathered around the grill while the girls were unpacking hot dog buns and condiments.

Shane noticed Avery excuse herself from her conversation with Cooper. Her arms wrapped tightly across her chest. She was quickly making her way toward the river. Should he go after her? He'd only wanted to get her attention; he'd never wanted to upset her.

"Please excuse me," he told Chelsea once he realized she

was trying to make conversation with him that had fallen on deaf ears.

He headed in the direction of the river and found Avery at the bank, hands in the back pockets of her jean shorts, kicking at a rock that was lodged into the mud.

"Hey, Ave. What are you doing down here?"

"I asked you not to call me that," she said, her voice filled with gloom.

"Is everything okay?"

Silence. "Yes, everything is just fine."

Even though it had been nine years, he still remembered what "just fine" meant. "Want to take a walk up the river with me? I remember seeing a good swimming spot in the canoe today, it's just up the trail a bit."

"I'm not going swimming right now. We're getting ready to eat. Besides, the water is too cold."

"Then just take a walk with me. I'd really like to talk to you." Shane made a praying motion with his hands, as if to say please, paired with his most genuine smile.

After a moment of hesitation, she started walking upstream in the direction he had pointed out. Shane fell in stride next to her, elated that she had actually agreed. Now that he had her attention, he had no idea where to begin. He swallowed hard to try to release the knot that had formed in his throat.

They walked in silence for a few minutes, Shane willing himself to focus on the beauty that surrounded them. The sun was low in the sky, and an amber glow filled the horizon. A bald eagle soared overhead, and they both stopped to watch the magnificent sight. It was quiet, other than the babbling river beside them, and Shane felt a wave of peace wash over him for the first time in a very long time. It was good to be home.

They came to a private clearing, and he pointed out a fallen tree to sit on. "After you." He held out his hand to help her get situated on the log. When she placed her hand in his, a charge passed between them.

51

"You have me here, Shane. What is it you want to say?" She turned to face him and looked him in the eyes. *Finally.*

"I—I just want you to know a few things." He ran his hands through his hair and tugged at the ends. Frustration rushed through him. He had to find the words. This was the moment he'd been waiting for. He'd planned long ago that if he ever made his way back to Arbor Shores, he would give Avery the apology and explanation she deserved. He'd been playing the words over in his mind since Dax called and invited him to be in the wedding, knowing at some point he'd have an opportunity to come face-to-face with Avery.

"First, I have to tell you, my leaving Arbor Shores—leaving us—was just as hard on me as it was on you."

"What makes you think it was so hard on me? Did Dax tell you that?"

"What? No, I just know you wouldn't be so upset with me if I hadn't hurt you. I know I did, and for that, I'm sorry. Believe me, if I could take that back, I would."

"Would you though?" Doubt filled her voice. "You really think you would've been happy if you'd stayed here and never became the huge rock star you are now?"

"I don't know. But for one, I'd still have you. Hopefully," he added when he saw the surprised look on her face. "Avery, I didn't leave to get away from you. It wasn't even so much about the music."

The look on Avery's face told him she wasn't buying it. But it was the truth, and if she knew the whole story, she'd understand. Wouldn't she? He studied her eyes and contemplated his next words. Should he be honest with her? They weren't even close anymore. Would she even believe him if he told her the secrets he'd been holding onto for years?

He took a deep breath. "For starters, my dad was really pushing me to work in the family business. I was feeling the pressure as the eldest of the Knox boys. There's nothing, and I mean nothing, I wanted to do less than go to work for my father.

I couldn't fathom the thought of staying home to attend college, and then being tied to a nine to five job. Much less being under my father's rule. That was Hunter's dream, not mine." It wasn't the only reason he wanted away from his father, but it was a start. Should he tell her the rest? Was this the time and place?

"I get that, but that would've given you a future if you wanted to stay." She sighed deeply. "But I'm not sure that would've been the best fit for you. Being a famous rock star seems to suit you." She looked away.

"Ave, I need you to know, it was not easy leaving." He reached for her hand and held it softly. "It was not easy leaving *you.*"

She turned back to face him. "Well, you made it look pretty easy. We had plans. You made promises. But you never spoke to me again. Not even when my fath—"

"I know, and I'm so, so sorry. I was young, and it hurt too bad to walk away and leave you behind. To walk away from us. But you were only a senior in high school. It's not like I could've taken you with me."

"I know that, and I always knew you would leave to pursue your music career, but you were supposed to wait for me. We had plans to leave together. When you left I thought you'd come back for me. I turned down Cornell University because you said you'd come back."

"Wait, you never told me you got accepted into Cornell. That was your college of choice. I remember you wanted to go there and study agricultural science more than anything."

"I never told anyone I was accepted. I knew if I went, it would be the end of us. I turned it down my senior year. I shredded the acceptance letter so my father would never find it."

She stood up and walked toward the water. He followed her and stood behind her. "I didn't know, Avery. You should've told me."

"Why?" She swung around to face him. "Would it have made a difference if you knew I gave up my dreams?"

"I had to leave when I did. I don't expect you to understand, but there are things you just don't know." Shane put his hands in his pockets and looked down at his feet.

"Well, you could've told me those things. Instead, you went off chasing your dreams, while I threw away mine."

There it was. The real reason Avery was so upset with him had finally risen to the surface. Guilt stabbed at him. What could he say? Was there any way to make it right?

"I'm sorry things ended the way they did, but you and I both know it wouldn't have worked. I was always on tour. You would've been all alone out in California. We were just too young to make it work, Ave. I'm sorry."

She huffed. "Do you feel better now that you got that off your chest?"

"No, I didn't do this to make myself feel better. I owed you an explanation and an apology." He took a step toward her, but she stepped back, keeping distance between them.

"You're too late, Shane. Nine years too late." She turned and started down the river toward the campsite.

"Please let me finish," Avery heard Shane call out to her.

Something in Shane's voice made her stop and turn around. She let her hands drop to her sides as she let out the breath she'd been holding since she turned to walk away. She didn't want to keep up this fight, but it felt good to finally say things out loud. She had waited for this moment for years. But now, she'd said what she needed to say and just wanted to get back to camp and crawl inside her tent.

"There's no reason to rehash things now, is there? After the wedding, you'll be leaving, and there's no telling when I, or anyone else in this town, will ever see you again. Please, just let me be."

"Fine. But answer me one question first." He moved toward

her and closed the distance between them, putting his arms around her waist and pulling her close.

It felt good to be in his arms. She still fit perfectly there. Should she allow him to hold her or push him away? As much as she knew she shouldn't get close, she found comfort in his arms, and right now she needed a hug. She needed *his* hug. "What's the question?"

"Do you still feel something between us? Be honest. You know how we were together. That doesn't just go away."

"Shane." She shook her head before resting it on his chest. What was she doing? She needed to be strong, but he smelled so good, his scent so familiar.

"From the second I saw you behind the desk at the resort, every feeling I've ever had for you came rushing back with a vengeance. Tell me you feel it, too," he whispered next to her ear. His warm breath sending chills up her neck.

Avery felt his grip loosen, and she picked her head up to look at him, their faces only inches apart. He brushed a piece of her hair away from her face and ran his thumb across her cheek. She closed her eyes and melted into his touch. How had he managed to make her feel like this? She had promised herself she wouldn't let him back in.

Soft lips brushed against her cheek, then slowly made their way to her mouth. She took a deep breath and put her hands on his chest. "What are you doing?" she whispered.

"I'm sorry. I got lost in the moment." Shane stepped back and held his hands up. "Tell me you don't feel something between us, and I'll walk away. If you look me in the eye and tell me that, I will leave you alone."

Avery forced herself to look away. She couldn't be strong if she looked at him. She couldn't look into his eyes and say the words she needed to say to make sure they didn't go back down a road with no final destination. He'd just said so himself. It wouldn't have worked when they were younger. So, how would it work now? He was always on tour, and her life was in Arbor

Shores. She was needed at the resort now more than ever. There was no sense in opening old wounds— wounds that had cut deep and took far too long to heal the first time around. She couldn't let him back in. No way.

"I don't feel anything anymore, Shane. I'm sorry to disappoint you." She turned quickly and started back down the river so that he wouldn't see the tears threatening to spill from her eyes.

CHAPTER 8

*A*very arrived back at the campsite more distraught than ever. She couldn't shake Shane's words from her mind or the feeling she'd had when he held her. She could still feel his strong arms wrapped around her, and she kept replaying the moment over and over.

Why was she fighting her feelings for him? Why couldn't she just let him know that she hadn't been able to get him off of her mind since he stepped onto the resort?

Because he's leaving, Avery. She never wanted to feel that pain again. She wasn't willing to break down the walls she'd built up around her heart—not for the Shane he'd become. He was famous now. He had a new life across the country in California. How dare he even try to rekindle her heart for the weekend when he knew he was leaving as soon as the wedding was over. The more she thought about him leaving, the more those memories of her heartbreak stabbed at her, and the more she vowed to stop thinking about him altogether.

Back at the campsite, everyone gathered and ate dinner. Afterwards, the girls sat around the picnic table and chatted with a bottle of wine while the guys played a game of cornhole behind the tents.

The sun was gone now and the sky was dusted with stars. The only light left was the glow of the fire and the flashlights they each carried. Dax swooped in and kissed Leila on the cheek. "Are you cold? Do you want my sweatshirt?" he asked.

"That would be nice. Thanks, babe." Leila looked up affectionately at Dax, and Avery couldn't help but admire their love for each other. She realized she, too, was getting a bit chilly, so she went to her tent and grabbed a hoodie before retiring to a chair by the fire. She watched as the boys piled wood atop the blaze, and poked and prodded at the fire as men do.

Cooper sat down beside her. "You look down," he said. "Everything okay with you?"

"I'm okay. Thanks for asking." She took a sip of her wine and gave him a half-smile before returning her gaze to the flames.

"Ok, well if you'd like to talk, I'm here," he offered.

"Thanks, Cooper, but really, I'm good. Just enjoying some downtime. I've been working a lot lately so I'm just trying to relax." She didn't mean to sound rude, but she wasn't up for small talk. A pang of guilt gnawed at her for being overly friendly with him earlier. Why had she done that? Was she subconsciously trying to get Shane's attention? If so, it had worked, but she'd given Cooper the wrong idea, and she felt awful for it. He got up and joined the other guys around the fire, which made her feel even worse.

It wasn't long before his spot was filled by Shane. "Listen, I'm not going to stay sitting here, I know you don't want that," he began. "I just thought I owed you an apology for how things happened by the river. I don't know what came over me, but I didn't have any right to try to kiss you."

"You're right, you didn't," she agreed in a soft tone. She had lost her desire to fight. Maybe it was the wine that had mellowed her mood, or maybe she was just tired altogether.

"Do you want me to sit somewhere else?" He looked at her with hopeful eyes. "Because I will get up and move right now."

She let out a soft giggle and a hint of a smile. "No, we can be mature adults and sit by each other, Shane." She took a sip of her wine. "I just want you to understand that I don't have any interest in being your weekend fling while you sweep through Arbor Shores. I'm sure you have plenty of groupies for that."

Before he could offer a rebuttal, Dax yelled from across the firepit, "Shane, when are you gonna play us a song? I saw you brought your guitar."

"Later, man. I'm not really feeling up to it right now."

"Come on, you have to play for us," Dax pressed.

"Please, Shane," Leila chimed in. "You can't say no to the bride!"

"All right. Let me grab my axe." He flashed Avery a grin. "This conversation is not over."

Avery didn't know if it was the second glass of wine, or the soothing sound of Shane's voice echoing through the campsite, but she couldn't take her eyes off of him as the light from the fire illuminated the features of his face. He closed his eyes to hit the high notes of the chorus, the rest of the time his eyes locked on Avery's as he sang.

Funny thing was, she'd secretly followed his music career quite closely, and she'd never heard this song before. Had he written it for her? There's no way he could make a song like this up on the fly, could he? Perhaps he wrote it for someone else? The final line of the song made her second guess that.

No matter how far I roam, with you, I'm always home ...

As the song finished, everyone clapped and a few of the guys let out a long whistle, cheering their friend on in their own private concert among the stars.

After Shane had finished, he moved to his tent to put his guitar away, and Avery decided to follow him. Was it the music?

The wine? Either way, she was ready to be alone with him. She had some things she wanted to say herself.

"Can we talk?" She was waiting outside his tent when he emerged.

"I would love that. Where do you want to go?" he asked.

"Do you have a flashlight?"

"Let me grab it." He went back into his tent and came out a few minutes later with a flashlight and a blanket. "In case you get cold."

It had gotten chilly, and she could use one more layer. He walked over to the picnic table and grabbed the bug spray, giving her bare legs a spray before doing his own.

"Come with me." He held out his hand to her, which, for whatever reason, she decided to take. They walked silently through the woods, and Shane guided her around tree stumps, pointing out exposed roots on the path with the light of the flashlight.

When they reached the opening at the river, the full moon shone down on the water, illuminating the area where they stood. Avery could feel him moving closer as she turned to face him.

"Something you wanted to talk about?" he asked, wrapping the blanket around her and pulling her close to him. She knew that grin. That was the look he had in his eyes the first time he'd kissed her so many years ago.

"I just wanted to say, how dare you come to town and try to wiggle your way back into my life when you know darn well you'll be leaving again." She knew her tone didn't match the toughness the words were meant to portray. It was growing harder and harder to stay upset with him. Especially wrapped in a blanket that carried his scent.

"We are two adults now." He pulled her even closer. "Yeah, I have to leave again, but that doesn't mean we can't make this work now that we're older. I think it's worth exploring, don't you?"

"Make what work, Shane? There is no us. You don't even know me anymore."

"I know you, Ave. I could go twenty years without seeing you, and I'd still know you."

"Oh yeah? How so?" She tilted her head to await his response.

"I know that you like your iced tea with two lemons and one sugar. I know you have a habit of chewing the inside of your cheek when you're deep in thought. I know that you'd rather spend an afternoon hiking alone than with a group of friends, and that your dream is to someday turn Arbor Shores Resort green."

Man, he was good. She'd always had plans to turn Arbor Shores eco-friendly. She'd even met with the Green Building Council. Now, all she needed was the funding. Still, she'd been environmentally conscious even as a teenager and everyone who knew her knew that side of her.

"There is so much more that you don't know," she told him.

"But that's the fun of it, right? Getting to know each other again? For the most part, I'm still the same Shane, and you're still the same Avery. We're just a bit older and more mature, that's all."

"Older, more mature, *famous.* You live in California, Shane. What would happen when you go out on tour?"

"We can make it work, Avery. You could come with me. What's really holding you here?"

She chuckled. "I won't be your groupie. And you know I can't leave my mother alone with the resort. I'm a lifer in Arbor Shores. Besides, I love it here. This is my forever home."

"But soon you won't have the burden of running the resort once Hunter acquires it. What will you do then?"

She pulled back and let the blanket fall from her shoulders. Did she just hear him right? She knew something was up when she saw Hunter leave her mother's office. Her heart plummeted.

What was her mom hiding from her? "What? What are you talking about?"

Shane's eyes widened, shock washing over his face. "Uh, you mean you didn't know?"

"Know what, Shane? Come on, spill it!"

"I assumed you knew. I really shouldn't have said anything." He rubbed at the back of his neck and threw his head back, looking up at the sky.

"Shane Knox." She pushed her chest up against his and pointed a finger at him. "I'm telling you right now to spill it. I have a right to know."

"All I know is that I went to my dad's, against my better judgement, and Hunter was there. It was a short visit that didn't end well, but while I was there, they mentioned that he was acquiring Arbor Shores Resort."

"No way." She shook her head in disbelief, refusing to accept his words. How could this be happening? "I saw him come out of my mom's office. She said he presented a business idea that she had no plans of entertaining."

"Well, from the way they made it sound, the resort is in trouble, and you know that if they want it, they will find a way to get it. I'm sure they will make a generous offer."

She took a step back. "You Knox men are all the same. You think because you have money you can just get whatever you want—"

"That's not fair. I have nothing to do with this. I don't even speak to my family. I was just telling you what they said. And, like it or not, when they want something, they do usually get it. Is the resort really in trouble?"

"The resort is just fine, Shane," she lied. "Don't you worry about the resort."

"Avery, please calm down. I didn't mean to upset you. I thought you knew."

Hot tears streamed down her face. The thought of the resort that had been in their family for her entire life going to Hunter

Knox, who was known for tearing down properties, panicked her. What would her mother do? The resort was all she had left of her father. What would Avery do?

"Dax can know nothing of this," she warned him. "Tell me you didn't mention this to him."

"I didn't know it was a secret, but no, I didn't say anything to him, and I won't. You have my word."

"I don't want anything to ruin this weekend for him. We'll just get through the wedding first. He can't know anything about this," she reiterated. And with that, she started back toward the campsite.

"Avery, wait," she heard Shane call after her, but she ignored his plea. She was upset, and if he knew best, he'd just leave her alone.

Avery was up by the crack of dawn. She'd barely slept the night before. Her sleeping bag didn't offer much padding from the hard earth beneath her tent, and she couldn't shake visions of Hunter Knox taking over the resort from her mind.

The resort had been in trouble for a while, and if they were going to save it, she'd need to do something drastic. She had a Fourth of July Jamboree planned for the following weekend, so that would surely bring some faces back to the property. The resort always hosted an after-parade party, when everyone in town would meet back at the resort for a BBQ since that's where the floats started and ended. This year, Avery decided to make it an all-day event and have the party go until the fireworks ended. She had to remind people why they should stay there for the summer instead of the new summer rentals in town. She had to somehow remind everyone why Arbor Shores Resort was the place where memories were made. But she wasn't even sure if people would come. She'd put flyers up all around town, and she'd placed an ad in the *Arbor Shores Beacon*, but would it be enough? She wished she could do something grand, something that would bring people from downstate or even out of state … but what?

She didn't have time to worry about it right now. She had to get back home, get showered, and get over to the resort to help her mother set up for the rehearsal dinner.

"Morning, Sis. Sleep well?" Dax emerged from his tent, stretching his arms high in the air.

"Like a rock." More like *on* a rock, but she didn't want her brother to know anything had kept her up. "What time are we heading back? I really need to get to the resort to help set up for tonight."

"Would you relax and enjoy the last bit of vacation you have? All you do is work." He ruffled her hair, something that had driven her nuts since they were kids.

"Dax, you know I can't leave Mom with all the set up for today."

"We'll be leaving shortly," he reassured her. "Hey, I saw you and Shane walk off holding hands last night. What's going on there?"

"Absolutely nothing. Just a bit too much wine, and a moment of weakness," she said, detecting the concern in his voice. As much as Dax loved both her and Shane, Avery knew he didn't want to see them back together. It was clear that everyone knew it could never work.

"He's leaving, Avery. Just remember that," he warned.

"I know that. I just said nothing was going on," she spat, more aggressively than she intended.

"Okay, okay. I'm just looking out for my kid sis."

"I'm only a year younger than you. I don't know why you still call me that."

He put his arm around her and pulled her close. "You'll always be my kid sis. And I'm always going to look out for you."

"Well, thank you, but I can look out for myself."

"Hey, speaking of which, I'd like to start helping out more around the resort." He gave her shoulder a squeeze. "I know I haven't done much lately. I've been in a funk since Dad died, and I've thrown myself into golf the past few summers. I want you to know, I'm sorry for putting so much on you and Mom. I have big plans for how we can bring some new life back to the resort this summer. Maybe when Leila and I return from our honeymoon, you and I could have lunch and discuss some ideas?"

"I would really like that." It was a nice thought, but two weeks from now might be too late. Still, she couldn't tell Dax that. Not until after his honeymoon, anyway.

CHAPTER 9

*A*fter the afternoon wedding rehearsal, Shane headed back to his cabin, ready for some alone time before dinner. He unlocked the door and was met by a wall of musty air. But that didn't bother him. He loved the rustic feel of the cabins. It sure was a nice change from the hotel rooms he'd slept in most nights while on tour. He went straight to the fridge and cracked open a beer, taking a long pull off the bottle.

He couldn't shake the way he'd upset Avery. He loved this resort; he'd made some of his best memories here. He wasn't thrilled about his family taking it over either, but Avery didn't seem to get that. She'd lumped him in as a typical Knox, and that hurt. He'd worked for the past nine years to forget that he was even tied to that family, and now he'd only been in town a couple of days and he was already associated with his brother and father's business antics. He didn't know if he should be hurt or mad, but the more he thought about it, the more he was teetering on the edge of angry.

He opened the sliding door and walked out onto the private deck that overlooked the lake. The cabin was just hidden enough in the woods that he got all the privacy he needed, yet the patch of trees in front of him was cleared to offer a full view of the water. He sank into a patio chair and put his feet up on the deck railing, taking in the towering pines that surrounded him as two hawks circled overhead.

He hadn't realized how much he missed his hometown until he returned. He couldn't get enough of the warm June air and the scent of evergreens that constantly surrounded him. He appreciated the simplicity of a small town and all the innocent fun that was to be had here. Why had he waited so long to come home? He was beginning to think he wasn't ready to leave on Monday as planned. He could use a little downtime to think about his next move. Plus, he needed to write some new songs, and this seemed like the perfect place to do just that. Sitting there on the deck, the blue sky overhead, was the closest he'd been to inspired since before his divorce.

Shane felt his pocket vibrate. He pulled out his cell phone and looked at the screen. It was James. He'd only been gone camping twenty-four hours, and his manager had called four times. Shane figured he'd better answer, or he'd just keep calling.

"Knox," he answered, putting the phone to his ear.

"Where have you been, Shane? I've been trying to call you."

"You know where I am, James. I'm at my buddy's wedding, remember?"

"You don't answer the phone when you travel?"

"I was on a camping trip. No reception."

"A *camping* trip? Where are you again?"

"Michigan. What's up?"

"Just reminding you about *The Aftershow* next weekend. How's the new music coming?"

"Yeah, about that. It's not going to happen, James."

"You're a songwriter, Shane, remember? God knows you haven't written anything in ages but you'd better come up with something. I'm afraid the future of Distant Union depends on it."

"What's that supposed to mean?"

"It means you've only had three hit albums. The songs are

getting stale, and people want new material. When I first signed you, you were on fire with your songwriting. You wrote hit after hit. What happened?"

It was true. When James had first signed Shane, he'd still been heartbroken over Avery—the kind of heartbroken that inspired great lyrics. But you couldn't force art. He'd rather write *no* music than bad music. Shane pushed off the chair and rose to his feet. He couldn't deal with James right now. The pressure of writing new material was too much.

"Listen, James, I really do have to go."

"Since you'll be in New York, I'm having your publicist set you up with a promotional tour," he continued. "You'll be there for the week so we're changing your flight. You'll fly from wherever it is that you are straight to New York on Monday instead of coming back to LA. You'll do appearances all week, then the band will meet you there on Saturday for *The Aftershow*."

"No. I don't want to do any appearances next week." Shane wasn't ready to think about leaving Arbor Shores to go straight to the city.

"I'll have Lori send you the flight info once the arrangements have been made." *Click.* The line went dead. Why wouldn't James listen? It was like Shane didn't even have an identity anymore.

Shane paced the deck to work off some steam, kicking at a stick that had fallen from one of the trees above. The last thing he wanted to think about was a new song. Not with the rehearsal dinner happening in less than an hour, and everything that had been happening with Avery. He tugged at the back of his shirt and pulled it up over his head, tossing it on the patio table before moving toward the door. Shower. Rehearsal dinner. That much he could manage.

He paused at the door. The cool breeze felt good on his skin, and slowly he began to calm down.

"Hey stranger, long time no see." A voice floated up his deck stairs, but it wasn't the voice he was hoping for. It was Chelsea, in nothing but her bikini top and a pair of jean shorts that couldn't possibly get any shorter.

"Hey, Chelsea. What are you doing here?" He wasn't in the mood for company.

"I'm in the next cabin over. I could hear you talking to someone, and you didn't sound happy. I thought I'd come see if I could cheer you up." She gave him a grin that spelled trouble. One that he was used to receiving from hungry women. He needed to stay far away from this girl.

"I'm good. I was actually getting ready to get in the shower so ..." How could he get rid of her?

A look of desperation flashed across her face. "The other reason I'm here is because my little sister is a huge fan. I was wondering if you would sign something for her. She's thirteen, and she has your posters plastered all over her walls."

Shane had a feeling she was lying. "Yeah, sure. I'll get you something before the weekend is over."

"It'll just take a minute. Did they leave a resort pad of paper and a pen on your nightstand? That will work." She looked up at him through long lashes. "Please?"

He hesitated and let out a sigh. "Okay. I'll be right back." He went inside to fetch the pad of paper and pen, and just as he did, the screen door slammed behind him. He turned around, and Chelsea was standing inside his cabin.

He picked up the pad of paper. "What's your sister's name?" Annoyance bubbled inside him. Why was she in his cabin? He'd been happy to leave his security detail behind when he came to Arbor Shores, but now he wished he had someone to help him block the door.

"Kayla," Chelsea said, as she sauntered closer to him. He scribbled something quickly and tore the paper from the pad.

"Here you go." He handed her the autograph. "I really have to get in the shower now. I'll see you tonight." He could see that look in her eyes, and he'd met enough groupies to know what was coming next. He put his hand on her back to guide her toward the door. When he finally got her on the other side of the door, she turned to face him, putting her hands on his shoulders.

"If you get lonely in here all by yourself, you know where I am." She leaned forward and kissed him on the cheek before he could shield himself from her advance.

~

Avery blinked hard. Did she really just see what she thought she had?

She had just snuck a bottle of champagne into Dax and Leila's cabin, so they'd have it waiting when they returned from their couple's massage at the spa, and she thought she'd head over to Shane's cabin to apologize for how she'd acted the night before. She knew she had said some hurtful things, and guilt was eating at her. Shane didn't deserve her ire just because he was a Knox. He was nothing like Hunter or his father, and she couldn't bear that she had said they were all the same. She owed him an apology.

What she hadn't anticipated was that he wouldn't be alone, and that Chelsea would be coming out of his cabin, him shirtless, her in a one-size-too-small bikini top. What's worse, she was certain she'd seen Shane and Chelsea kiss. Avery had ducked behind a thick oak tree as they emerged from the cabin, but she saw the lean in, and she was sure it was a kiss. She also had an idea about what they had been doing *inside* the cabin in the middle of the afternoon.

She put a hand over her torso, feeling like she'd been punched in the gut. It was a similar feeling to seeing pictures of Shane and Naomi when they were dating, although this stung worse. Why was he trying to rekindle with her if he was going to turn around and hook up with Chelsea? Feelings of betrayal engulfed her heart.

She should've known better. As a rock star, this was probably how his life was on a daily basis. Different girls every night or day, anytime he wanted one. A relationship with him could never work. What was she thinking to actually consider giving it a shot? As upset as she was about the resort, she'd be lying if she said the main thing keeping her up the night before hadn't been her attempts to piece together what a relationship with Shane might look like if they gave it another chance. Now she felt foolish. For a brief moment, she had wanted nothing more than to have him back in her life. Now, she wanted nothing more than to have him out of Arbor Shores once and for all.

Avery ducked into the employee bathroom to change out of her khakis and polo shirt, her standard work uniform, and into a navy cocktail dress and nude slingback heels for the rehearsal dinner. She had fifteen minutes before it was set to begin, and she'd just finished with the table settings, checking on the wait-staff, and making sure the harpist she'd hired was settled on the veranda where the sunset dinner was scheduled to take place.

She pulled her hair out of her ponytail and gave it a shake, her long wavy mane looking effortless. She touched up her face with powder and applied a coat of lip gloss and a dab of blush to each cheek.

She emerged from the bathroom and saw the light was still on in her mother's office. She checked her watch. Not nearly enough time to have the conversation they needed to have, but Avery couldn't help herself.

She strode over and knocked on the open door. "Knock, knock," she said, announcing herself.

"Avery, you look beautiful. Did you have fun on the camping trip, dear? I haven't had a chance to talk to you all day. It's been quite crazy around here."

"It was great," Avery said shortly, taking a seat across from her mother's desk. It looked like she was crunching numbers. "What are you doing?"

"Ah, just some end of the month balancing, but it can wait." Meredith quickly closed the books and flipped over the calculator, shoving it all in the desk drawer.

"When were you going to tell me?"

"Tell you what, dear?"

"About Hunter Knox acquiring the resort?" Avery asked pointedly.

Meredith took a long sigh as if she were buying time to select her words. "With all that's going on this weekend, that's the last thing you need to worry about. We'll discuss it on Monday, how's that?" She got up from the desk and turned to grab her shawl from the coat rack.

Avery studied her mother. She had already changed for the evening as well. She had a timeless beauty with her hair piled up in a loose bun. But age lines cut deep in the corners of her eyes, likely from the long hours she'd been keeping at the resort, and she looked thinner than ever. "So, it's true?"

"No. Well, yes and no. He made an offer, a generous one at that, but I'm not interested in selling if there is any way to keep the resort. Your father would turn over in his grave if this resort was turned into condos."

She walked over and cupped Avery's face with both hands and looked into her eyes. "Don't worry yourself with this. I'll think of something."

Avery stood. She knew there was no reason to keep the conversation going when they had to get to the rehearsal dinner. But she also knew there was no way her mother could save this resort on her own.

She would have to come up with something herself. And quickly.

CHAPTER 10

*U*pon entering the veranda, Avery could see everyone was already seated at the tables she had set for the evening. Luckily for her, she'd been in charge of the seating chart so she put the bride and groom at a round with their families. Leila's parents shared a table with Meredith and Avery, along with Leila's grandparents who had flown in from New York. The Cookes had a small family and both sets of grandparents were deceased, so that only left Meredith and Avery for Dax's immediate family.

Avery took her seat, feeling Shane's eyes on her from the next table over. Her plan was to avoid him until the wedding was over and keep herself busy with the festivities. Tomorrow was the wedding, and as the maid of honor, she had lots planned to help the bride on her big day.

The gentle chords of the harp filled the evening air. High above, small white lights were strung over the veranda. The tables were covered with white linens, and the centerpieces were simple—fresh-cut lilacs that filled the air with the sweetest scent. There was a light chatter among the guests as everyone got to know one another or caught up with the family they hadn't seen in a while.

Leila and Dax handed out gifts to their wedding party. The guys received golf balls and tees that had the wedding logo stamped on the side, and the bridesmaids received embroidered beach towels in the wedding colors—the perfect gifts for a resort-themed, summertime wedding.

Toward the end of the meal, Dax and Leila stood up and made a toast, taking turns to thank everyone for traveling to their wedding and spending their special weekend with them. When it was Dax's turn for the mic, he added, "I'd especially like to thank Shane Knox for flying all the way from California to be here with us."

The crowd clapped, and Shane nodded his head in Dax's direction. "I know we don't get to see each other much, you being famous and all," Dax added with a playful tone, which then turned serious, "but you'll always be like a brother to me, and Leila and I would like you to know how much it means to us that you're here." Dax was starting to choke up, and it was apparent to Avery that Shane being here meant more to her brother than she had realized. "Now, get ready for tomorrow morning when I kick your butt on the golf course!"

The guests laughed, and Dax and Leila took their seats as the staff brought around coffee and dessert. The evening was winding down, and it occurred to Avery that this was the perfect time to give them the bride and groom gift she'd had custom made for them—personalized champagne flutes for tomorrow's reception. She stood up and snuck inside to retrieve them from behind the front desk. With all the chatter, hopefully nobody noticed that she'd slipped out.

Shane watched as Avery stood from her seat and excused herself from the table. Where was she going? He couldn't take his eyes off of her in that dress and the way it accentuated her curves in all the right places. He watched as she headed back inside the resort. Without skipping a beat, he got up to follow her. He trailed behind her as she walked through the lobby, stopping to adjust a floral arrangement that had fallen flat. That gave him the opportunity to catch up to her.

"Avery, wait," he called out. She turned at the sound of her name, but quickly went back to toying with the arrangement.

"Shane," she finally said, her tone icy. If she was still upset about the news regarding the resort, he could understand that. Standing in the grand lobby of this lodge, with cathedral ceilings towering over them and floor-to-ceiling windows that looked out over the veranda, it was hard to imagine Arbor Shores without it. The place was iconic. The thought of his family tearing it down tugged at his heart. He felt like he'd grown up here with the Cookes.

"You look beautiful tonight." Shane flashed her a smile, but she didn't seem to notice.

"I'm busy, Shane." She headed toward the front desk, but he fell in stride behind her. He wasn't going to let her blow him off.

She went behind the desk and fetched a box with a ribbon wrapped around it. Just as she did, two young twin girls, who looked to be around eleven, came running up to him in the lobby. "Oh em gee! Are you Shane Knox?" one asked, and they both erupted in giggles.

"Yes, girls, I am." *Bad timing.* He noticed the girls' parents watching from afar with smiles on their faces, and he knew he was stuck.

"See, I told you!" one said to the other. "Can we, uh, can we *please* get your autograph?"

These girls were too sweet for him to be annoyed, although he was mildly frustrated with the timing of it all. "Let me see if I can borrow a pen from the front desk."

He figured Avery must've heard because she tossed a pen and a pad of paper on top of the counter and headed back toward the veranda. He was stuck doing the fan thing, and now other people in the lobby had come over and started asking for pictures.

By the time he'd finished with the crowd and went back out to the veranda, Avery was nowhere in sight. The only one left at her table was her mother.

"Mrs. Cooke, it's so nice to see you." He approached Meredith and leaned down to kiss her on the cheek.

"Shane! It's so nice of you to come all this way for the wedding," she said, her warmth making him feel immediately welcome. She had always treated him as one of her own, and Shane appreciated it, especially after his own mother left. "Sit down. I haven't had a chance to chat with you yet." She motioned to the seat next to her.

"Do you know where Avery went?" he asked, taking a seat.

She paused and gave him a smile. "Probably to her cabin for the evening. She's staying at the resort this weekend to make things easier with the wedding and all. Big day tomorrow!" she added, beaming with excitement.

"Do you know which cabin she's in, by chance?"

She leaned closer with hopeful eyes. "Are you two rekindling old flames?" There it was—no beating around the bush with Mrs. Cooke.

"I'd just like to talk with her. She seems upset with me. I didn't know she wasn't aware of Hunter acquiring the resort. I'm afraid I'm the one who spilled the beans. I'm sorry." He lowered his voice so nobody could hear, but Dax and Leila were off saying goodbye to their guests, and nobody else was left at the table.

"Ah, yes. Well, how could you have known?" She paused to take a sip of her coffee. "This place is Avery's life. You know, she was always a daddy's girl. After her father passed, she made it her mission to help me keep this place running. I believe in some way she's still trying to make him proud."

"Well, you've both done a nice job with it."

"I'm afraid that's not been enough." She set her coffee cup

down on its saucer and turned to him. "Truth is, this place could use a facelift. The cabins need a fresh coat of paint, and there are countless repairs that need doing. But none of that really matters if we can't get people to the resort. It seems families just want to rent summer homes now. Fewer and fewer want to stay here each summer."

"That's a shame," Shane said. "I have so many wonderful memories here. Maybe you just need to remind them why Arbor Shores Resort is so great in the first place."

"Well, there's a lot of work that would have to be done first, but I think you're right. People have just forgotten."

"Avery mentioned a Fourth of July Jamboree next weekend. Maybe that's your opportunity?"

"Yes, that's her plan, bless her heart. She is trying."

That gave him an idea, an idea that could save this resort from his brother once and for all. He rose to his feet.

"Which cabin did you say she was in?"

"Number four." She gave him a wink before rising from the table. "Good luck, Shane."

He wasn't sure what she meant by that. "Good luck?"

"My daughter's been guarding that heart of hers since ..." she hesitated. "Never mind. I hope the two of you can become friends again." She smiled sincerely before walking toward Dax and Leila.

Friends. That was an excellent idea. That was an angle he hadn't yet considered, but right now he was willing to take whatever he could get.

Shane could hear the crickets off in the distance, their melody in full sync, as the cool evening air enveloped him. He followed the glow of path lights down to the cabins at the bottom of the hill. Cabin number four was at the opposite end of the shore from where Avery had placed him. *Figures.* Man, she really didn't seem to want much to do with him. He was bound and determined to change all that if his plan worked.

He approached the cabin, and through the window he could see the amber glow of a lamp inside. He watched her through the window for a moment, sitting in an armchair across from the fireplace, a glass of red wine in her hand. She looked deep in thought as she gazed into the flames. Boy, did she ever look beautiful. She had taken off that stunning dress and changed into a pair of boy shorts and a form-fitting tank. Her hair now piled on top of her head in a messy bun, she looked more relaxed than ever. He knocked softly and ducked behind the door.

"Who's there?" she called out, without getting up.

"Ave, it's me. I have something important to talk to you about."

"Go away, Shane." Her tone didn't make him feel hopeful.

"It's about the resort. I just need five minutes. You're going to want to hear this."

There was a pause, and a deafening silence that seemed to last an eternity. Finally, he heard the creak of a chair scraping the wood floor, and a moment later the door swung open. His eyes made their way up her body, causing her to quickly turn away to grab a blanket from the back of the chair and wrap it around her shoulders to cover herself. He couldn't help but stare. This was the love of his life, after all. He knew every inch of her, but up until that moment, he had forgotten just what it did to him. Suddenly, he felt seventeen again. She always had driven him wild, but now she had morphed into a woman, and he longed to be close to her.

"Get an eyeful?"

"Hey, I didn't tell you to open the door in your underwear," he teased.

Her cheeks turned the most adorable shade of pink, and she seemed flushed. At least he could still get a rise out of her. That had to count for something.

"What are you doing here?" she asked, sinking back into her chair.

"May I have a drink with you?" He closed the door behind him.

She hesitated. "Wine is on the counter. Glasses are in the cabinet to the right of the sink. Whatever you have to tell me better be good."

He poured himself a glass and took a seat in the armchair next to her. Both were facing the fire, so he turned his chair to face hers and leaned forward.

"First, just let me say, thank you for agreeing to talk to me." He took a sip of wine and put it down on the table between them. He had to choose his next words carefully. "I have an idea for how you can save the resort."

She let out an exasperated sigh. "Why do you care, Shane? I mean, really. Was this your ploy to get in my cabin? Haven't you had enough fun for one day?"

He wasn't quite sure what she meant by that, but he chose to ignore it. "I was just talking to your mom and—"

"Talking to my mom? Why are you talking to my mom about the resort?" Her face held a mixture of hurt and anger.

"I just sat down to say hello and catch up with her. We got to talking about the resort, and it got me thinking. People have just forgotten what makes this place great. You just need to get them back here so they can remember."

"Well, thank you for figuring all of that out for us, Shane. I hadn't thought of that." Her words dripped with sarcasm. So far, things weren't off to a good start.

"What if, for your Fourth of July Jamboree next weekend, I put on a concert here? We could get people to come from all over Michigan. We could pack this place. Your cabins and the main resort would sell out, and—"

"I can't afford you," she said, cutting him off. "*We* can't afford you. It's a terrible idea."

"I'm not looking for compensation. I just want to help."

"Why?" She put her wine down and sat upright in her chair, fire in her eyes. It half turned him on and half scared the life out of him.

"Because I just want to be your friend, Avery." He'd try that on for size to see how it fit. "I understand I hurt you, and you have no desire to get back together, but if we could find a way to be friends again ..." He searched for the right words. "I just want you back in my life."

~

"If you want me back in your life, you're going about it the wrong way." How dare he come to her cabin after he spent the afternoon with Chelsea in his. As much as she wanted to tell him what she saw today, it wasn't her place to question him about his afternoon antics. They weren't together, and she had made it clear she didn't want to get back together. He was free to do whatever he wanted with whomever he wanted. Even though the thought of that twisted her stomach in knots, she chose to swallow what she saw between him and Chelsea and keep it to herself.

"How am I going about it wrong? I want to help you bring life back to the resort again." His voice changed, and she could tell he was getting upset. He stood up, and she couldn't help but admire how handsome he looked in his dress pants and button-down pressed black shirt. He had loosened his tie and unbuttoned a few top buttons. This was a look you wouldn't expect to see on him since he had the rock star persona going on most days. He cleaned up well, and this look suited him.

"I'm just saying, for someone who claims he wants to be back in my life, you sure didn't waste any time with Chelsea." *Shoot.* She didn't want to go there. She didn't want to sound pathetic or let on that she had any feelings left for him at all, but her jealousy got the best of her. She rose to her feet, ready for the battle.

"With Chelsea? What are you talking about?" His voice rose.

"I saw you two."

"Again, enlighten me, Avery. I've avoided her all night. I don't know what you're talking about."

"This afternoon." There it was. "I saw her leave your cabin half dressed. I saw the kiss." Well, that was a half-truth. She saw the lean in, but she was sure it had ended in a kiss.

"Ave." He reached out and put his hands on her shoulders and looked into her eyes, a serious look on his face. "It's not what you think."

"It doesn't matter. It's none of my business. I'm sure it's a regular occurrence for you nowadays." She turned away to escape his grasp.

"What is that supposed to mean?" he asked, his tone filled with anger.

"Like I said, it doesn't matter. Please leave."

"Fine." He headed toward the door and turned around to face her. "But I didn't do anything with Chelsea. She came to my cabin and asked for an autograph for her sister and pushed her way in. I got her out as quickly as possible. There was no kiss. She pecked me on the cheek before she left but that was it."

"It doesn't matter," Avery repeated.

"You're right, it doesn't matter because the truth is I'm single, and I can do whatever I want." *Ouch.* "You don't want anything to do with me anyway, so why do you care?"

"Get out," she demanded. She could feel tears welling up in her eyes, and she refused to let them spill in front of him.

"Fine, I'll go. But I didn't touch her, and that's the truth. You can accept it or not. But my offer still stands about the concert. The ball's in your court."

The screen door slammed behind him, jolting her with a dose or reality. What had she done? Why did she have to confront him about Chelsea? There was no denying that she had feelings for him now. *So much for playing it cool.*

His words stabbed at her heart as she replayed them in her

mind. Hot tears escaped the corners of her eyes. What if he was telling the truth, and she just ran him off after his generous offer? As much as she didn't want to admit it, she knew having Shane Knox headline at the resort was the one thing that might save it once and for all. Shane sold out every venue across the US and Europe. He'd just offered her the greatest gift imaginable, and she'd treated him terribly.

She flopped onto the couch and let the tears flow until she cried herself to sleep, just like she had so many nights since he left her long ago.

CHAPTER 11

*A*very woke to the sound of birds chirping outside of her cabin. A dull ache pulsed behind her eyes, and she wasn't quite sure if it was the wine, the crying, or a combination of both that was to blame. Glancing at the clock, she knew she'd better get in the shower and get up to the main lodge. The women were having a spa day with pedicures and facials, followed by hair and makeup as they pampered the bride on her special day.

On the bright side, she wouldn't have to see Shane until the ceremony. The guys had a 9:00 a.m. tee time, and then they'd likely end up at Ripples to unwind afterward.

One look in the mirror at her swollen red eyes and she was grateful for a spa day with the girls. Not so excited to spend the day with Chelsea, but she loved Leila, and as the maid of honor, she was fully prepared to put her own issues on the back burner and give Leila one hundred percent of her attention.

She dabbed some concealer under her eyes, but her efforts were no match for the dark rings. She pulled her sunglasses out of her purse and committed to wearing them as long as she could get away with it. She'd had embroidered robes made for all the ladies in the wedding party with their name on the front pocket and *bridesmaid* stitched across the back. Except for hers which said *maid of honor*, and Leila's that, of course, said *bride*. She wanted to get up to the bridal suite before anyone else so she could set them out for each of the ladies.

She loaded the boxes containing the robes in the golf cart she had taken to her cabin the night before. She stuffed her toiletries in a duffle bag along with her shoes for the wedding and headed up the hill. Her dress for the ceremony was already waiting inside the suite.

Avery could tell it was going to be a gorgeous day. She'd always loved summer mornings at the resort, but this one felt particularly magical. The temperature wasn't forecasted to get above the upper seventies all day, and there wasn't a single cloud in the powder blue sky. Perfect weather for outdoor nuptials.

Avery pulled the golf cart to a stop in front of the main lodge. She decided she'd better check on how the set up was coming along before heading to the bridal suite. She found her mother out on the veranda. The florist was there decorating the pergola, and Mrs. Cooke was showing the event staff how to place the chairs for the ceremony. A beautiful backdrop of Lake Michigan filled the horizon behind the pergola. It was already looking whimsical. Avery loved this venue for a wedding, and she secretly longed to get married there herself one day. She just regretted that her father wouldn't be there to walk her down the aisle. A sadness tugged at her heart.

"Avery, what are you doing here? You're off today, remember?"

"Just checking to see if you need any help with anything."

"Your duty is to the bride today. I've got this covered." She flashed her daughter a reassuring smile.

"Well, you're the mother of the groom so you shouldn't be doing all of this yourself."

"I'm fine. I have more than enough help today." She put down her clipboard and walked over to her daughter. "So, did you have a visitor last night?"

"Ah, yes, thank you for that," she said dryly. "Now I know how he found out which cabin I was in." Avery gave her mom a pointed look.

"Avery, I don't see why you two can't just be friends. What happened between the two of you, that was a long time ago. People grow up, and life goes on. It's time to let it go."

"Let it go?" Avery felt herself growing frustrated with her mother, and she didn't want that. Not today.

"You two once loved each other very much. He left to pursue his dreams, and look what he's made of himself. You can't fault him for that. Now, I know it hurt you when he left, but first loves always hurt. They wouldn't be called first loves if they lasted forever."

"You and Daddy were first loves. It lasted until ..." she let her voice trail off. She knew it would be hard for her mother to be alone today. Her father should be with them; it just wasn't fair.

"Yes, but times are different now." She patted her daughter's hand. "I'm just saying, give him a chance to make things right. This is your opportunity to get some closure. You've been carrying this heartache around for far too long."

Avery started to open her mouth in rebuttal but caught herself. She felt foolish because she knew her mother was right, even though it hurt to hear her words.

Her mother gave her a comforting smile before heading in the direction of the ice sculpture that had just arrived. She was left standing in the middle of the veranda, secretly wishing it was her that was getting married today.

The day was flying by. After their pedicures and facials at the spa, the ladies retired to the bridal suite for hair and makeup. A knock on the door indicated the champagne had arrived, and with an hour until the ceremony, it was time to give a toast to the bride and wish her well. Avery poured a few sips into each flute, and each of the ladies gathered around and raised their glasses.

"Leila, I just want to say that there isn't anyone on earth I'd rather see my brother with, and I'm so glad the two of you found each other. I'm honored to welcome you into our family. You're already the sister I never had, and I wish you both a lifetime of happiness."

The ladies all cooed and clinked glasses. Leila took a sip before setting hers down to wrap Avery in a hug.

"Thank you for everything, Avery. You've really gone out of your way to make today special."

"Shall we get you into that dress?" Avery motioned toward the beautiful white flowing gown that hung on the back of the closet door.

She took the dress off the hanger and held it open and low to the ground so Leila could step into it. Leila placed her hands on Avery's shoulders to brace herself as Avery shimmied the dress up her body and then moved around to the back to zip it up.

"So, what's going on with you and Shane?" Leila asked.

Avery was taken aback by the question, and the rest of the girls in the room fell silent from their chatter, as if awaiting her response.

"What do you mean? There's nothing going on between us." She did her best to stay cool as she knelt to dig under the bustle and fiddle with the fastenings.

"I was just curious if you two had given in yet. Seems like you've been fighting it since he got here." Leila shot her a playful smile over her shoulder.

"Nah, that all ended a long time ago." Avery rose to her feet and immediately went to work securing a ringlet that had sprung loose from Leila's updo.

"So, you're telling me you have no interest in Shane?" Leila tested her in a tone that told Avery her future sister-in-law wasn't buying her story.

"Not in that way, I don't. We were kids. Those feelings died long ago." She didn't see any harm in fibbing. Technically, they weren't family just yet.

"Then you don't mind if I go for him?" Chelsea chimed in from the corner, a hungry smile spread across her face. "I think there may be something between us and—"

"Suit yourself," Avery said, perhaps a little too quickly, still fidgeting with Leila's hair. She tried to back pedal because she could feel all eyes on her, and she didn't want to let on to her annoyance. She did her best to plaster on a smile and soften her tone. "Like I said, that was over long ago. He's fair game." Those may have been the most painful words she'd ever spoken. Did she just give Chelsea full rights to pursue her ex? Did she just put him on the market for the redheaded goddess that could clearly get any man she wanted?

At least now she would see just how much Shane really wanted her back in his life. The way he handled this situation would tell all. Was this a test? Perhaps, but she was certain Chelsea would be going for it now, and Avery knew she would have to up her game. For some reason, she'd believed him when he said that nothing had happened between him and Chelsea, so there was no reason to stay mad. If she wanted to see if there was a future between them, then she needed to stop pushing him away. Perhaps they could make it work.

Somehow. Some way.

The morning with the guys had been a blast. Even though Shane finished twelve over par, he couldn't remember a time when he'd enjoyed a round of golf quite as much. Maybe it was the perfect summer day, or being back home with his boys, but he felt like himself here, and he hadn't felt like himself in years. He barely had time for fun anymore. It seemed all he did was tour, make media appearances, and sleep off the long nights until it was time to get up and do it all over again. His life had become monotonous, and that's something that had started to chip away at his soul long ago.

He stood next to his best friend at the front of the processional, as the guests were ushered one by one to their seats. A violinist played a soft tune that drifted through the afternoon air, and a warm breeze tickled his skin and rustled the leaves in the trees behind him—a soothing and familiar sound that spelled out *home*. Any minute now, the bridesmaids would start walking down the aisle. He couldn't wait to see Avery.

Once all the guests were seated, the music changed, and the bridesmaids began their descent from the side of the main lodge, down the aisle. One by one, they all took their spots; the last to emerge was Avery. She was breathtaking. Her hair was in a loose updo, and soft tendrils hung down and swept her bare shoulders. She was wearing a form-fitting, pale pink, satin-gown with spaghetti straps. She walked slowly, a stunning smile on her face, as she took turns acknowledging each side of the audience, nodding to familiar faces while holding her bouquet. The closer she got to the front, the harder it was for Shane to breathe. He couldn't remember a time when she'd ever looked so beautiful. She took her place at the front, across from him. She met his gaze for a moment and gave him a soft smile before looking toward the end of the aisle. He'd told her he wanted to be her friend, but could he ever settle for just being friends? How could he have her in his life and not have all of her?

Another change in music indicated the bride was set to walk down the aisle, and the crowd rose, all eyes awaiting Leila, except for Shane's. He couldn't take his eyes off of Avery.

As the ceremony ensued, he wasn't sure if it was the nuptials, or listening to Dax and Leila recite their vows, but he was hit with a wave of nostalgia, and he couldn't help but wonder what his life would be like today if he'd stayed in Arbor Shores. Would it be him and Avery walking down the aisle? There was no way to ever actually know; he'd thrown that chance away when he left, but he sure didn't mind the thought of it.

And now, he wasn't even the same person he was back when he was with Avery. He had loved her so freely back then, without guarding his heart, the thought of being hurt never crossing his mind. After what he'd been through with his divorce, he wasn't sure if he'd ever be capable of having a love like he'd shared with Avery when they were young. Now they were both jaded—him because of Naomi, and Avery because of *him*. Knowing that tore a hole in his heart.

As happy as he was to be there, every part of the wedding was a constant reminder of his own failed marriage. He was damaged from what Naomi had done to him. And while he knew in his heart Avery was not like Naomi, would he ever be able to trust again and give her the love she deserved? Who was he kidding? He was damaged goods, and she deserved more from a man.

As Dax leaned in to kiss his bride, Shane got a clear shot of Avery, who was only a few feet across from him. Finally, as the officiant announced the couple as husband and wife, Avery's eyes met his, and he could see tears had gathered in their corners. Were those tears for him? Was she having the same thoughts that he'd been having? Probably not. They were likely tears of joy for her brother.

It was time for the bridal party to follow the happy couple back to the lodge. As the maid of honor and best man, he and Avery were supposed to walk arm in arm. The crowd cheered for the bride and groom as they made their way back to the lodge, stopping to kiss a few times for their guests to take photos.

The wedding director gave Shane and Avery a nod, cuing that it was time for them to walk. Shane stepped forward and held out his arm for Avery. She slipped her delicate arm through his and flashed a quick smile in his direction. Was that smile genuine? Or was she was just putting on a show for the crowd?

The crowd stayed standing and continued to cheer as they walked past them and back up to the lodge. It felt so good to have Avery beside him. He could smell a hint of her sweet scent that always warmed his insides. He wanted to tell her how beautiful she looked, but he knew she wouldn't hear him with all the cheering going on. So, he just walked her as slowly as possible, reveling in having her by his side where she belonged.

As soon as they were out of sight of the guests, she released his arm and wandered over to hug her brother and Leila. It wasn't long before the photographer was corralling the wedding party for photos. They all took turns in different group poses around the property with the bride and groom. First a picture of the groomsmen with just the groom, then with the bride, then with both the bride and groom and the bridesmaids.

That lasted for nearly an hour, and when it was over, so was the cocktail hour for the guests who were now all seated in the ballroom waiting for the announcement of the wedding party. One by one, the DJ announced each bridesmaid and groomsmen pair, and they joined hands and entered the ballroom as the guests rose to their feet to welcome them with applause.

"Please welcome Avery Cooke and Shane Knox!" It was their turn. He held her hand high in the air for all to see as they entered the ballroom. The feeling of her soft hand in his shot adrenaline through his entire body. Avery seemed to be enjoying herself as they strolled through the room together, which lit him up. They stopped at the long table that sat in front of the floor-to-ceiling windows. It was time to take their seats on either side of where the bride and groom would be sitting.

"Ladies and gentlemen," the DJ announced, "please stay standing, and join me in welcoming the bride and groom, Mr. and Mrs. Cooke!" The crowd cheered as Dax and Leila entered, and the DJ transitioned the music to their wedding song. They danced slowly, gazing longingly into each other's eyes as the guests took their seats to enjoy the show.

When their wedding song ended, the DJ quickly transitioned into the next slow song. "Now, if I can have the wedding party join the bride and groom on the dance floor." This was the moment Shane had been waiting for—his chance to dance with Avery.

Each groomsman and bridesmaid linked up with their respective partner for a slow dance. He had Avery in his arms now, his hands resting on the small of her back while hers rested on his shoulders. She hadn't looked at him yet, and he knew this was his chance to apologize for the way they had ended things the night before.

"You look beautiful, Avery," he whispered in her ear.

"Huh?" She looked up at him through dreamy eyes.

"You're absolutely stunning."

"Thank you." She gave him a bashful smile as her cheeks flushed. That was a good sign. She seemed to have lost some of the fire that was in her the night before. He couldn't decide which look drove him crazier—feisty Avery ready to take on the world or soft Avery who was slowly melting in his arms? He wanted their dance to last forever.

"I'm sorry about last night, Ave." He pulled her close to his chest and held her a little tighter so he could speak softly into her ear. He could feel eyes on them, and he didn't want people to make out his words. Privacy was something he respected, but got little of.

"I'm sorry, too." He wasn't expecting that. Were they finally going to put down their dukes and stop fighting this thing that was happening between them? "I shouldn't have—"

"Shh, you don't have to say anything more." He leaned his head down so he could look into her eyes. "You're forgiven," he said, flashing her his best smile. No need to rehash another word. Right now, he just wanted to keep Avery in this mindset.

He felt her body soften into his as she leaned closer and rested her head on his chest. It was a moment of surrender, and all of his doubts disappeared. He decided right then and there that he never wanted to let her go. Not ever.

CHAPTER 12

*A*fter the scheduled dances, dinner, and his witty best man speech, the guests were in full-on dance mode. Shane took the opportunity to sneak out onto the veranda while many of the guests, along with the bride and groom, were doing the electric slide in unison. Where had Avery disappeared to? He was determined to find her. He wanted to get her alone and talk with her, and this was the perfect time.

To his delight, he found her at the edge of the terrace, looking off over the lake. She appeared to be lost in thought. She'd taken her hair down, and she looked like an angel as it blew softly in the wind.

"Nice night," Shane said.

She looked startled as she turned to face him. Avery met him with a smile as she rubbed her crossed arms. The air had cooled to the low sixties, and her dress looked as thin as a nightgown. He slid his tuxedo jacket off and slipped it over her shoulders. She accepted the gesture. He couldn't believe the shift in Avery since last night, but he was relieved. Did this mean she believed him about Chelsea? He wanted so badly to ask, to make sure she knew he would never do something like that, but he didn't want to bring it up. Things were going far too well at this point.

"Walk with me?" he asked, holding his hand out for hers. She looked down at it and hesitated, but then, to his delight, she placed her hand in his and allowed him to lead her away from the lodge and down the path toward the shoreline.

"You're quiet tonight," he finally said, breaking the silence as they paused to remove their shoes at the sandy shore.

"My father should be here," she finally said. Shane felt like an idiot for not putting two and two together. Of course, she was sad about her father not being at her brother's wedding.

"I'm sure he's looking down from Heaven, proud of all you've done for Dax and Leila today. I'm sure he's here in his own way."

She gave him an appreciative smile.

"Have you given my offer any thought?" he asked.

"It's a generous offer, Shane, it really is, but aren't you scheduled to leave on Monday? The Jamboree isn't until next weekend."

"I can change my flight," he said quickly. But could he? His manager would have a fit, and his publicist had already scheduled him for appearances all over New York City. He'd kept getting text notifications on the golf course. He'd eventually switched his phone off and left it in his cabin. "I was thinking I'd stay for the week, maybe do some work around here. If you'll have me?"

"Work?" She laughed. "What kind of work are you planning to do?" she asked with amusement in her voice.

"I was thinking we could spend the week fixing the place up a bit. I can help paint the cabins. Not all of them need it, but a few do. And that fence down at the Beach Club needs repairing."

"You'd want to do that?" she asked, stopping to turn to him.

"Why not? It's been awhile since I've been home, and honestly, I'm enjoying being back here. I could use a break from LA. I'd welcome some manual labor for a change."

He thought he saw her face fall at the mention of LA. It was almost as if any hope building between them was killed at the mere mention of it.

"I'll think about it," she said after a few moments, and he hoped that meant yes. As long as he didn't screw this up.

"Walk the shore with me?" He held out his hand for her once again. She slipped hers back into his, and he led her up the shoreline, in the opposite direction of the resort. Soft waves lapped at their feet, and a billion stars twinkled above them.

Finally, he stopped and turned her toward him, wrapping his arms around her and pulling her close for a long hug. She laid her head on his chest and allowed him to hold her.

"Do you realize this is the spot where we had our first kiss?" he said softly by her ear.

She picked up her head and looked around and then looked up at him. His hand traveled up her back, and his fingers tangled in the hair at the nape of her neck. Gently, he guided her closer as he leaned in and brushed her pillow-soft lips with his.

"Shane—" Their lips barely touched before she pulled back.

"I'm sorry," he said. "I guess with the wedding, this night, our spot. Something just came over me."

"It's not that I don't want to kiss you, but not tonight. It's been a hard night for me, and I'm really missing my dad. Right now, I could really just use a friend."

"You got it." He tilted her chin up and met her eyes before pulling her back in for a hug. How could he be so senseless? It's just that whenever she was near, he couldn't help himself. He was ready for things to go back to how they once were, and being with her felt so natural. Even after all of the years of not seeing each other, it felt like they could pick up right where they left off. But could they? It's what he wanted. He was sure of it. But he was starting to realize, with Avery, it was going to take time. And time in Arbor Shores was something he didn't have much of.

"We'd better get back to the wedding. People are probably beginning to talk."

"Ah, let them talk." He held out his hand for her once again. She gave him a sideways look.

"What? Friends hold hands. I mean, sometimes." He flashed her an innocent grin and she gave in, allowing him to hold her hand as they walked back to the lodge.

Shane tossed and turned all night, unable to shake the feeling of Avery's soft body in his arms. Adrenaline had kept him awake. He hadn't been this excited about a decision in a long time, and the fact that she might allow him to stay the week and help fix up the place meant she'd more than likely decided to move forward with the concert.

A thought jarred him. What would he tell his manager about staying in Arbor Shores for the week? What would happen when he missed his appearances in New York? Media appearances were one thing, but the gig with *The Aftershow* for Distant Union was a great opportunity for any band. Would skipping it be detrimental to his career and possibly the band's future with their record label? He was willing to deal with the consequences of his own choices, but the one thing he didn't want to do was let down his band. He'd have to talk to them before this plan of his went any further.

After a long hot shower, he put on a pair of board shorts and a plain white tee and headed to the main lodge to meet the rest of the crew. They were all going to Ripples for brunch, and then they planned to spend the day on the beach. Leila and Dax were not scheduled to leave for their honeymoon until Monday morning so that they could spend a full day of fun with their out-of town-guests. He was looking forward to a relaxing beach day, especially because it meant spending the day with Avery.

Ripples was the place to be on Sundays. It's where most of Arbor Shores gathered for brunch, and with the beach volleyball courts right in the sand off the back deck, guests could either play in the Sunday tournaments or watch from the patio. They had a party of eight reserved at a long table overlooking the beach, thanks to Rylee.

"Hey, guys," Rylee said with a big smile, approaching the table and leaning in to hug Leila and Dax. Shane wondered why someone like Rylee was still single. Probably because she worked so much to take care of her son. It was too bad she couldn't find someone special; she really was a great girl and he'd always gotten along well with her. She'd be perfect for his guitarist, Axel. Nah, on second thought, that was no life for someone like Rylee. She deserved more. But then, didn't Avery deserve the same?

Shane was hoping to position himself next to Avery, but she took the seat next to Leila, and Cooper had planted himself next to her. *Of course he did.* The guy wasn't going to give up. Could he blame him? Avery was a great catch. Unfortunately, this landed Shane next to Chelsea, and she took every opportunity to touch his arm in her flirtatious manner. He noticed Avery kept an eye on him. He adored her little jealous streak. It gave him hope that she still had feelings for him somewhere deep inside her, whether she was willing to admit it or not.

Avery got up to excuse herself. "I'm going to the Bloody Mary bar," she announced, holding up the glass that Rylee had delivered, awaiting its toppings.

"I'll go with you," Shane said, rising to his feet and meeting her with his own glass. They shimmied their way through the crowd and into the restaurant, where a massive table was set up along the back wall with all the fixings from bacon to pickles and blue cheese stuffed olives.

"They sure do put out a nice spread," Shane finally said, dropping treats into his glass as they both built killer Bloody Marys. It soon became a competition to see who could build the best one. By the end of the line they both had a mountain of fixings towering out of their glasses. They compared master-pieces and laughed.

"So nice to see you two kids back together." Shane recognized that voice. He didn't even have to turn around to know Hunter had walked up behind him.

"Who are you calling a kid? You're *my* little brother, remember?" Shane said, knocking his brother's arrogance down a notch. Hunter was dressed in his best. Didn't he ever just kick back and relax? It was Sunday, after all, and Shane doubted his brother was coming from church, so what was with the sports blazer at the beach? Sometimes he wondered how it was possible they had the same genes.

Hunter turned to Avery. "I hope your mother has given my offer some thought. It will expire soon. It's a good offer for the two of you, and it'd be a shame for you to miss out." Shane could see the heat rising in Avery. He knew what was about to go down, and this time, he welcomed it. He contemplated putting Hunter in his place, but he knew Avery could handle herself in this situation, and to be honest, he was looking forward to the show.

"Actually, Hunter, I'm quite certain we won't be accepting your offer. We'll be sending an official reply in the morning," Avery said, taking a sip of her drink and staring him square in the eye. Shane could tell she was trying her best to keep her cool, but if he knew Avery, he also knew that would only go so far, and his brother was on thin ice.

"When was the last time you took a look at the financials?"

"Excuse me?"

"The financials. Clearly, you have no idea how bad it actually is. I've already talked to your bank, and unless you can come up with a steep investment very quickly, you will go into foreclosure. You can take my offer and walk away with a nice nest egg, or you can lose the resort and walk away with nothing. Either way, Knox Enterprises will end up with it. It's up to you."

Shane watched as Avery's face flushed with anger. How dare his brother talk to her like that. He had just opened his mouth to give Hunter a piece of his mind when Avery stepped forward.

"Actually, you won't be acquiring the resort. We'll have all the money needed to pay up the loan within the next few weeks. Unfortunately for you, Arbor Shores is staying in the Cooke family." She gave him a smirk. Now it was Hunter's turn to show signs of anger.

"And how do you plan to do that? With your little Fourth of July Jamboree you have planned? I've seen the flyers around town. Do you actually think that is going to raise the kind of money needed to save your resort? Clearly you have no idea just how bad of shape you're in. You and your mother have to let it go, Avery. It's time to allow someone to come in and make something of that property."

"That's enough, Hunter." Shane stepped forward, closing the space between him and his brother, but Avery had put down her glass and stepped forward to meet Hunter eye-to-eye.

"Two things. One, don't ever speak of my family again; and two, Shane's hosting a concert next weekend, so I don't think I'll have any trouble filling my *little Jamboree*."

Shane nearly choked on an olive he'd popped into his mouth. Did she just say what he thought she did? Did that mean she'd agreed to allow him to have the concert?

Hunter turned to face Shane. "Really?" he asked dryly. "*You're* putting on a concert at the resort next weekend?"

"You have a problem with that?" Shane set his glass down, fully prepared to put his brother in his place if need be.

"Man, I don't know how you can even call yourself a Knox," Hunter snapped. "You go ahead and play your pro bono concert to save your girlfriend's resort, but I promise you, you can kiss your place in the Knox family goodbye if you do."

"I said goodbye to being a part of the family long ago, Hunter," Shane said coolly. "Ain't no skin off my back."

"You do this, and I'll make sure that you're out of Dad's will once and for all."

"Go right ahead. Last time I checked, I make my own money, and I don't need my daddy's money to get through life, unlike some people I know." Shane knew that one would sting. He always suspected Hunter might be the sole heir of the Knox fortune, although it was never officially announced, but he also knew that deep down Hunter had always wanted to make his own money. That's why he was always looking for these side real estate deals to try to impress his father. Hunter lived to impress Carter Knox.

"Gentlemen, I'm going to need you to take this outside." Big John had approached the threesome and inserted himself between the two brothers. A crowd had formed around them, and all eyes in the room were on the Knox brothers.

"No need," Shane said. "We're done here." He stared down his brother, jaw clenched, fists balled at his sides, as if to dare him to say another word. It was clear that Hunter knew when to stand down to his older brother, because he turned and walked away. "Avery, shall we?" Shane said, holding out his hand for her. She took it and allowed him to guide her through the crowd.

When they were out of the view of the prying guests, he turned to her. "So that means you'll take me up on my offer? I'm going to play at the resort next weekend?"

"You bet your bottom you are," she said through gritted teeth, clearly still seething from the run-in with Hunter. "And Shane," she said, squeezing his hand and looking up at him, her face softening. "Thank you." She finally let the anger flush from her face.

"Anything for you, Ave." He was thrilled that he'd broken down the walls she had built up and was just glad he could do something to help her and Meredith with the resort. Now, his only issue would be what to tell his manager and his band.

"I don't know how I'll ever thank you for this," she said, looking down at her flip-flop as she drew an imaginary circle with her foot.

"Well, there is one thing you could do." His eyebrows danced with his words.

~

"And what's that?" Avery asked Shane, intrigued by his comment.

"Chelsea is coming on strong. You'd be doing me a real favor if you acted like we were back together for the rest of the afternoon."

"What?" she laughed, assuming he was joking.

"She's all over me, Ave," he said, holding his hands up innocently. "Come on, she leaves tomorrow. It's just one day of pretending, and it will keep her out of my hair. I'd really like to relax and enjoy my Sunday without prying her wandering hands off of me every five minutes."

Avery was growing tired of watching Chelsea paw at Shane herself, and the idea wasn't half bad.

"I suppose I could do that *since* you are going to such lengths to help me," she agreed. "But only for today," she added quickly with a pointed finger.

"Of course. Tomorrow we'll go back to you playing hard to get." He grinned at her with his sexiest of smiles.

She playfully slapped him on the arm. His arrogance came peeking through at the most opportune moments, but not a Hunter-level arrogance. It was more like a sexy confidence that only Shane Knox could pull off. One that secretly drove her crazy. In a good way.

He held out his hand. "Shall we?"

Avery took his hand and headed back to the table. It felt good to be by his side. It was almost as if he'd never left, and they were picking up right where they'd left off. Even if they were just pretending. Something was happening between them that couldn't be denied, and she was running out of will to fight it.

When they reached the table, the looks on everyone's faces made it clear they had some explaining to do. But she didn't mind that everyone in the vicinity was whispering and probably making up their own version of Avery and Shane's story.

Perhaps it wouldn't be so bad to fake a relationship with Shane after all. In fact, it was the most natural feeling she'd had in a very long time.

"Well, look at this," Leila sang in approval. "Looks like the two of you are finally getting along."

"She finally stopped fighting it," Shane announced, kissing the back of Avery's hand that he was still holding.

It was showtime; everyone at the table had stopped mid-chew to check them out as they approached the group hand in hand. She met her brother's gaze, disappointment flitted across his face. Avery looked away quickly. She didn't need a lecture from her brother right now.

"What can I say?" Avery responded. She didn't quite know what to say, and the looks were making her uncomfortable. "It's hot out here. Anyone up for a game of volleyball? I think net three is open."

Everyone gathered their things, and Avery could see Chelsea sulking out of the corner of her eye. It was obvious she was not pleased about the match between Shane and Avery, and it secretly made Avery gloat. Every time Chelsea touched him, Avery had wanted to scream. She doubted she would've made it through a full afternoon if it hadn't been put to a stop.

Plus, she was enjoying the idea of having him as a boyfriend for the day, although she'd have to avoid any chance of kissing. She knew Shane, and he'd take that chance if he thought he could get away with it. That part she wasn't quite ready for. At least, not yet. Her defenses were weakening though; she was slowly running out of reasons to avoid his lips.

The crew enjoyed an afternoon of fun in the sun. Once evening set in, the guys built a small fire in one of the beach firepits, and everyone gathered around. Shane had brought his guitar and played and sang while everyone listened; he grew quite a crowd once people caught wind of the action.

Watching how Shane always drew such a crowd, Avery wondered if she could handle a life with him now that he had this new level of stardom. It seemed he couldn't go anywhere without being stopped or gawked at. As someone who loved her privacy, that would prove to be a challenge for Avery.

Pretending had started out fun, but after a few hours in, it was messing with her head. It hadn't been as easy as she'd originally thought it would be. Having him so close to her made it impossible to ignore her feelings, but she also couldn't ignore his fame. People everywhere knew who he was. It was giving her a glimpse of what a future would be like with him. She wanted to believe she could handle it, but she wasn't so sure. She was sure she loved that Shane took every opportunity he could to put his arms around her, hold her hand, or kiss her gently on the forehead. That part felt good. Better than she had anticipated.

When Shane finished his song and put down his guitar, Avery leaned over and whispered into his ear, "I have to go soon. I have to be at the resort early tomorrow."

"I'll take you," he offered with a smile.

"I drove myself here, remember?"

"Well, I'll walk you out then."

The couple rose to their feet and Avery said her goodbyes to Dax and Leila who were scheduled to leave for Bimini the following day. This would be the last time she saw the newly-weds for two weeks.

"Avery, thank you so much for everything. You really made our wedding day special." Leila leaned in and gave her new sister-in-law a long, appreciative hug.

"You two have fun in the Bahamas, and be safe!"

"Be good to my sister while I'm gone." Dax slapped Shane on the back and gave him a one-armed hug. Avery watched the interaction and knew Dax was giving his best friend a warning, in his big-brotherly way. She was just thankful he hadn't given them a hard time about their "relationship." Perhaps he could see that she was happy today. Even though Dax was overprotective, she knew he only wanted the best for her.

"I'm glad you've decided to stay the week."

"Me too, man. I just wish you were going to be here. But enjoy your honeymoon."

"Yeah, I'll take sipping margaritas on an island over painting cabins, but you two have fun with that!" Dax teased. Then his tone turned serious. "Think you'll be back this way again soon? When will I see you again?"

"You're going to be seeing a lot more of me. I promise you that," Shane said to Dax, but he stared at Avery as he spoke the words. He took Avery's hand in his as she turned to say goodbye to the rest of the guests, even Chelsea.

"I'm happy for you two. It's clear that you really do belong together," Chelsea told them both as she took turns hugging each of them. Guilt flooded through Avery's system. She could tell Chelsea meant her words, and now she felt terrible for faking this relationship. She'd never wanted to hurt her.

"Thank you, Chelsea." Avery gave her a genuine smile, and the two parted ways. At least they'd leave on good terms. Not that she was ever likely to see her again since Chelsea was flying home tomorrow.

Shane walked Avery to the parking lot, holding her hand the entire way, long after the group could no longer see them. When they reached the car, he turned to her and said, "Thank you for today. I had fun with you."

"Yeah, me too." She was starting to soften, and knew she had to pull herself together. "Tomorrow it's back to business as usual. No need to keep up the fake relationship after everyone leaves."

"Unless you wanted to?" he asked with a hopeful grin.

"There's no use in pretending to be something we're not

unless it evolves to that. Let's just take it one day at a time and see where this takes us."

"Well then, I'll see you in the morning, boss. I'll be ready for you to put me to work."

"See you then," Avery turned and began to open the door to her car, but she felt Shane push it shut. As she turned to face him to see what he was doing, he leaned in and pinned her gently against the car with his body. One hand on the door, he leaned in as if he were going to kiss her. With his other hand, he brushed his thumb along her bottom lip.

"What are you doing?" she tried to whisper, but her voice cracked.

"I've been dying to kiss you, Ave." His voice was low, his breath warm against her cheek, as he leaned in to whisper in her ear, "Ever since I got here, I've wanted nothing more than to feel your lips on mine."

"Shane ..." she started, but her voice trailed off. Her legs were getting weaker and weaker. She was running out of fight with this man.

"Just one kiss, Avery," he whispered softly. "And then we'll know."

Her eyes fell to his lips, so close to her own, and she began to close her eyes. She did want the kiss, more than anything. But she didn't want her heart to break all over again. She wanted to be certain this could work before they took it too far. She straightened her back, placing a hand on his chest to create space between them. "I already know, Shane."

Before he could say anything more, she leaned forward and dusted a kiss to his cheek. She turned and opened the car door, whispering a brief goodbye before she got in and backed out of her parking spot, leaving Shane alone to watch her tail lights disappear in the distance.

CHAPTER 13

$\mathcal{S}$ hane woke to the sound of a lawn mower off in the distance, the morning sun shining brightly into the cabin windows. For the first time in a long time, he was up with the sunrise. Some mornings, he was just going to bed at this time when on tour. He had to admit, it felt good to be up at this hour with energy and something important to do for the day. He never thought he'd be so excited to paint cabins.

He made a pot of coffee and took a cup out on the patio to enjoy the quiet morning. Directly in front of his cabin, a long dock called his name. He'd been dying to jump in the lake since arriving here, but he knew his body was no longer used to the frigid waters of Lake Michigan, having been in California for so long.

He wasn't sure if it was thoughts of Avery that he needed to clear from his mind, or the nostalgia of being back home that was affecting his logic, but before he could contemplate his decision, he put down his cup, removed his shirt, and jogged down the dock like a kid before diving off the end.

The water was frigid but rejuvenating, and energy surged through his system. He swam out as far as he could before he felt himself tiring, and then turned to head back to the dock. He was pretty far offshore now, but he could see a figure on the end of his dock—a figure in a pale-yellow sundress, that, make no mistake, was Avery.

"Good morning," she greeted him with an amused grin as he pulled his wet body back onto the dock. He noticed her eyes scanning his body. He had nothing on but his board shorts that he had slept in.

"Good morning, boss."

"I was coming to make sure you were up before I head to the main lodge." She still wore the grin as if she was pleasantly surprised to see him enjoying the lake.

"Of course I'm up. I can't wait to get started. What's my first task?"

"Well, I'm going to have to go into the city and get the painting supplies. Do you want to come with me?"

"There's nothing I'd rather do today than pick out paint with you," he teased, but deep down it couldn't have been closer to the truth.

"First, I need to tell my mom about the run-in with Hunter. I'll let her know about the concert so we can begin selling tickets. You're sure you want to do this?"

He was sure he wanted to, but how was he going to break it to his publicist and manager that he wouldn't be headed to New York today for a week of scheduled appearances? How was he going to get out of *The Aftershow* on Saturday night?

His manager had arranged for a private jet to pick Shane up, and it was scheduled to arrive at noon. When Shane didn't get on the plane today, everyone would find out. "There's nothing I want to do more," he said with a smile, but deep inside he had a gut feeling he was making a life-altering decision. Still, watching Avery's face light up, he knew he couldn't let her down.

"Thanks again, Shane. This really means a lot, and I just want you to know, I appreciate the gesture."

"Say no more. Now, go share the news with your mom, and I'll get a quick shower. Meet you up there in twenty?"

"Sounds like a plan." She gave him the sweetest smile before turning to walk back to the golf cart. He watched her walk away, grateful that he was finally getting somewhere with her, and no matter what, he wasn't going to allow anything to screw this up.

But first, he needed to talk to his band.

Shane's first call was to Sulley. "Hey, bro, what are you doing awake already?" Shane asked when he heard Sulley answer. It was the crack of dawn on the west coast, so he'd expected to leave a message on his voicemail.

"Believe it or not, I'm with Jax and Axel, and we're stuck in dreaded traffic on the 101. Lori and James have us scheduled for media appearances all freakin' day, starting with *The Morning Show*."

"Oh, man, well, that's kinda why I'm calling. I'm supposed to leave today to go to New York for some PR of my own."

"We're really gettin' sick of this, Shane. This isn't fun anymore, ya know? It's not what it used to be. We just wanna play our music, and James won't get off our backs."

"I hear ya, man. Well listen, I was thinking about sticking around here this week and blowing off these appearances in New York. I wanted to run it by you guys first."

"Oh no, if we are stuck doing this so are you!" Sulley yelled. Shane couldn't tell if he was serious or teasing. "Wait a minute, the girl is there, isn't she? The one you wrote all those sappy love songs for that you've had us singin' for years?" Now he could tell Sulley was teasing.

Shane ignored the question. "Here's the thing. I have a friend in trouble here. I thought I'd do her a favor by singing some songs at an event she's hosting on Saturday. Problem is, that's the same day as *The Aftershow* appearance."

"Answer the question, Shane. Is it *the* girl?" Sulley asked before smashing his horn and yelling profanities about a blinker.

"Yeah, it's her," Shane admitted. Sulley knew him all too well.

"Hang on, let me run all this by the guys."

Shane waited for what seemed like several minutes and many muffled horn honks later.

"Do whatcha gotta do," Sulley said, when he came back on the line.

"But what about *The Aftershow*?"

"So what about *The Aftershow*. The label isn't going to drop us for turning down one media appearance. James is just trying to strong-arm ya. Tell James we've decided as a band to turn it down. He can't make us all go. Besides, Jax just found out his girl is pregnant, so I think we'll be doing a bit of celebrating this weekend, if you know what I mean."

"Man, you guys are the best. Tell Jax I said congrats."

"All I know is if you're blowing off your media appearances today, we're turnin' this car around. We might as well all go down together, aye?"

"I'll give James a call later and give him the news. Right now, I have somewhere to be."

"Sounds good," Sulley said.

Shane heard a final horn honk before the line went dead. He just shook his head and laughed. He sure did love those guys, and he appreciated their never-ending support. He should have known that's how they'd respond. They were as close as brothers. Heck, he was closer to his band than his actual brothers, and now he knew he wasn't the only one in the band growing tired of the lifestyle and the demands of the music business. As much as Shane loved music, the label had taken the fun out of it for him. For all of them.

Maybe it was time for a change.

~

Avery headed to the main lodge to find her mom, but she wasn't in her office. Maybe she was coming in late? She left a note scribbled on a notepad on the desk.

Going into the city with Shane to get supplies. Don't know when I'll be back. Decline Hunter Knox's offer. I have a plan that will save the resort.

Love, Ave.

She grabbed the keys to the company pickup truck and headed to the front to wait for Shane. Right on schedule, she watched him jogging up the hill. She tilted her head to the side to enjoy the view. He was wearing faded blue jeans and a plain white tee. He looked casual and as handsome as ever.

"Ready?" she asked as he approached the top of the hill.

"Ready, boss." He winked, wiping the sweat from his brow.

"I figured we'd take the company truck so we can put the supplies in the back."

"Sounds good to me. Are the stores even open this early?" If memory served him, nothing in the area opened before ten.

"Not yet, but I figured I'd get some breakfast in ya before I put you to work."

"Now that sounds like a plan. I'm starving."

"Then, I figured we'd take a ride up the coast before we head into the city. It's been awhile since you've been home. I thought you might want to get out of Arbor Shores, and enjoy this beautiful day."

"As long as I'm with you, Ave, I'm happy."

She tossed the truck keys to him. "Wanna drive?"

"Sure." He walked around to the passenger side to open the door for her, holding out his hand to help her into the truck. He always was a gentleman, and she wasn't sure where he'd learned his chivalry, but she suspected it was from his grandfather whom he was always close to before he passed when Shane was sixteen. It certainly didn't come from Carter Knox.

They stopped and had breakfast in a small fishing town about twenty minutes north of Arbor Shores. They grabbed an outdoor table for two overlooking the harbor, and they watched as fishing boats left the docks for the day. After breakfast, they continued heading north up the tree-lined coast, and Avery kicked off her sandals and put her feet on the dash, the open windows letting in fresh morning air. They listened to classic rock on the radio, and Shane sang along.

"Is that old lighthouse still up at North Point?" he asked.

"It sure is. They closed it to the public several years back, so you can't get to it by the main gate. You can still get out to it, but you have to park down a side road and then walk up the coast for about a quarter of a mile."

Shane looked at her and grinned. "Take a walk with me?"

"You mean, to the lighthouse?"

"I'd love to see it."

She thought to herself for a moment about all that needed to be done at the resort, but something about taking a walk up the shore to the abandoned lighthouse with Shane was calling out to her. Plus, she hadn't seen it herself in years.

"Okay, up here about a mile, you'll see a small opening. Turn left onto the dirt road, and then park anywhere on the side of the road."

Shane followed her directions and parked the truck on the wooded road. They walked a short way to an opening that landed them on a deserted beach, then headed north up the shoreline. Shane stopped every few minutes to look for Petoskey stones, a native stone to the area that was commonly found on the shores of Lake Michigan. His excitement was infectious.

"Wow, it's even cooler looking now that it's abandoned," he said as they grew closer to the lighthouse. "Can you still get inside?"

"I don't think so. And even if you could, I don't think it's a good idea."

"Chicken?" he challenged her as he started jogging toward it. The lighthouse jetted off into the water on a rocky base, and the two had to climb those rocks to reach it. Once atop, Shane tried the door, but it was locked. He disappeared around the other side, and Avery scanned the area to make sure nobody else was nearby. She was already a bit nervous that they were trespassing, and now he wanted to go inside the abandoned lighthouse that had been closed for years? She had to admit, this was the most excitement she'd felt since she was a teenager when they used to sneak around so Dax wouldn't find out they were dating. When he finally did catch them, he wasn't happy. But after a few months he realized he could either spend time with them together, or Shane was going to keep disappearing to spend time alone with Avery, so he dropped the protective older brother act and gave them his blessing.

"Avery, over here!" she heard him yell from the other side. She met up with him to find he had opened a side door.

"Shane! What are you doing? We can't go in there. How did you even get that door open?"

"I pushed." He grinned. "Go to the top with me? I bet the views are amazing from up there."

"If we get caught, we are going to get into some serious trouble."

"Are you always this much fun?" he teased. "What happened to that fearless girl I used to know?"

"She grew up and got responsible. At least I can say that for one of us." But her comment fell on deaf ears as Shane disappeared inside. Avery couldn't help but follow him. The adrenaline of sneaking into the lighthouse was exhilarating, and she didn't mind the thought of being alone with Shane at the top.

She followed him in and closed the door behind her. A musty smell greeted her as she made her way up the creaky stairs to try to catch up to Shane, who was halfway to the top.

"Shane!" she hollered up in a soft yell as if someone would hear her. "Wait up, there are cobwebs everywhere!"

"Be careful on these stairs," he yelled down as he waited for her, allowing her to pass him so she would be in front of him. As she passed, he put his hands on her waist to steady her, setting off a chain reaction in her body. He always had a way of making her feel safe. "Here, you go ahead of me so I can catch you if you fall."

"I'm not going to fall." She gave him a playful smile, but she was comforted knowing he was behind her.

When they reached the top step, both of their mouths dropped in awe. The view of Lake Michigan from the top of the watchtower was spectacular. The lake went on for what seemed like an eternity, and the 360-degree views of the area were stunning. Unable to see across, the massive lake disappeared into an abyss of blue until it melted into a different shade from the cloudless sky. The watchtower was about ten feet in diameter, with an opening for the staircase in the middle, making it a tight fit for two people. Avery clung to a brass railing near the window. She felt Shane come up behind her and wrap his arms around her waist, enveloping her in the sweetest embrace.

She turned her body around to face him, and he kept his arms around her. She could feel his warm breath as he leaned in and cupped her cheek with one hand. She leaned into it, allowing him to caress her face.

"I've missed you, Avery." His voice was low. She closed her eyes, taking in the moment. She had a feeling he wanted to finish the kiss that nearly started last night outside of Ripples, and she couldn't think of any reason to stop him.

He moved his hand to the back of her neck, sensually combing his fingers through her long chestnut hair, sending shivers down her arms. He moved his hand back to the nape of her neck, and she could feel the gentle pull as he guided her closer, pausing to look deep into her eyes when their mouths were only inches apart. She parted her lips and looked up at him in surrender. Both of his hands moved to either side of her face, and he drew her even closer, so their lips were only centimeters apart.

The anticipation drove her wild, and she longed to feel his lips on hers. As her eyes began to close, she noticed his had drifted shut as his soft lips brushed hers, gently at first, as if to test her response, until finally she released whatever fight she had left and clasped her hands together behind his neck. She pulled him in, begging the kiss to go deeper. Heat rushed over her body as he wrapped his strong arms around her, pulling her closer. His mouth was so warm and his lips soft and inviting. She hadn't been kissed like this in years. She hadn't been kissed like this since ... *Shane.* It was as if they were having their first kiss all over again. But this was far better than their first kiss. There wasn't any awkwardness between them this time. In this moment, Avery knew her mouth was made for his.

"Hey, who's up there?" They heard a yell from down below, and they both pulled apart and looked at each other, frozen with shock before bursting into giggles.

"Oh no," Avery whispered to Shane. "What do we do?" Silenced and wide-eyed, they stared at each other and waited.

"I said who's up there!" the yell came again.

"I guess we're going to have to face the music. I'll do the talking," Shane assured her as he led her to the stairs. "Be careful." Avery's knees were still weak from the kiss, and now she had to walk down those stairs?

When they reached the bottom, they were met by a park ranger, and from the looks of him, he took his job quite seriously.

"Outside, both of you. Now." He was plump but older, and Avery couldn't help but notice he reminded her of her father. "This lighthouse is closed to the public. What are you doing out here?"

"This is my fault, sir," Shane began. "You see, I haven't been here in years, and I wanted to check out the view from the top. I take full responsibility."

"How did you even get in there? This door was sealed."

"Actually, it just pushed right open. It wasn't sealed when we got here, sir," he said. Avery suspected that was a fib, but then again, she wasn't there when Shane opened it.

113

"I'm going to have to write you both a citation for trespassing. What's your name, son? Why do you look familiar?"

"Shane Knox, sir."

"Well, I'll be darned, you are Shane Knox, aren't ya?"

"Yes, sir."

"What are you doing in North Point? Aren't you some big rock and roll star now?"

"Just visiting, sir. For the first time in a long, long time. So please, if you need to write a citation, I'll take it. She didn't have anything to do with this. Last time I was here, this place was open to the public."

"Well, you must've been gone for quite some time."

"Yes, sir. Nine years."

"Nine years! Well, yes, the lighthouse was open back then, but it's since been closed. You could've hurt yourselves in there." The man was softening.

"We're really sorry. It won't happen again," Avery chimed in with her sweetest voice possible, plastering an innocent look on her face. The one she used to give her father when she'd get caught coming in after curfew. Being with Shane made her feel alive again.

"Well, I suppose I could let you kids off with a warning, just this one time. Under one condition."

"Anything," Shane responded.

"I'd like to get your autograph. The guys down at the pub are never gonna believe this story otherwise."

"Sure thing, but not on that!" Shane pointed to the man's citation pad. They all laughed, and Shane signed a notepad the man pulled out of his front pocket, and they were on their way.

"Shane Knox, I told you that was a bad idea," Avery said, scolding him playfully.

"Well, I think it was a great idea." Shane smiled, grabbing her hand to hold as they walked down the shoreline back toward the truck.

"You nearly got us into trouble with that great idea of yours."

"Ah, we didn't get into any trouble. And Avery ..." he stopped to face her, looking deep into her eyes. "Honestly, that was the most fun I've had in a long, long time."

"Somehow, I find that hard to believe."

"Well, believe it," he said, pulling her close for a hug as he placed his chin on top of her head. She nuzzled into his chest and they both stared out at the water.

"We should really get going soon." She finally looked up at him, breaking the moment. "We need to get the supplies and get back to the resort."

"We will, in a minute." He guided her chin up gently with his fingertips, before he leaned down to finish what they'd started in the lighthouse.

CHAPTER 14

*T*hey arrived in the city and decided on a warm taupe for the cabins with dark brown trim. After gathering all the painting supplies Shane would need, they loaded it all in the back of the truck and headed back to Arbor Shores.

They'd both been giddy like school kids the rest of the morning, teasing and flirting like crazy, but now on the ride back to the resort, Avery was quiet. Shane wondered what was on her mind as she stared out the passenger window. Man, how beautiful she looked as the wind blew her hair wildly. She was making it hard for him to behave in that yellow sundress.

"Penny for your thoughts?" he asked, breaking the silence.

"Oh, sorry. I was just thinking about what Hunter said."

"About buying the resort? That's not going to happen now," he assured her.

"No, the part about my mom and I letting the place go."

"Ave." He leaned over to place his hand on her knee. "The resort is great. You're doing the best you can. Hunter was just being hurtful."

"Nah, he's right. I feel as if I've let my father down. It shouldn't have come to this point. We shouldn't even be in a situation where we could lose the resort." She looked down and smoothed out an imaginary wrinkle in her dress. "When he was alive, it filled to capacity every summer. The same families came back every year, and they would always reserve their cabins for the following year before they left. Now we struggle to fill even half of the cabins, and this is the busiest time of year in Arbor Shores. The resort is failing."

Shane was sure he'd heard a tremble in her voice with that last line, but he couldn't see her eyes as she was gazing out the window.

"We're going to change all of that."

"We don't know that." She finally turned to look at him, her eyes brimming with tears. "Sure, your concert will pack the place, and we'll make enough to save it from foreclosure, but then what?"

"I'm not sure, Ave. But I know you, and you'll figure this out. *We'll* figure this out."

"*We* will figure this out? You are leaving soon. After the concert, *I'll* be left to figure this out, and Arbor Shores will just be a distant memory to you once again."

Now he was getting to the bottom of what was really bothering her. Was it really what Hunter had said? Or was it that they were finally getting close again, and the sobering reality of him leaving had just hit her? He wasn't ready for this conversation. Not yet, anyway. But perhaps it was time.

"That's not fair, Ave. Like I said, we'll figure this out. We don't have to figure it out today, but we will before the week is over. I know we can make this work."

"Do you really think this could work, Shane? I mean, let's be realistic."

"You've already decided our future for us? We haven't even talked about it yet. We're just getting to know each other again."

She stared out the window. "The reality is, you are leaving. You're a famous rock star. Not to mention, you live in California, and I'm never leaving Arbor Shores. My life is here.

Everyone knows long distance doesn't work, and I don't have any interest in trying to make a relationship like that work."

"Well, I don't know what's going to happen after this week. We haven't even gotten that far yet, but I do know that I'd like to try." Shane flipped off the radio and a deafening silence filled the truck. Was she right? Was this relationship impossible to make work with his career and the distance between them? He had been so happy all day, thinking he was getting his Avery back. He wasn't going to lose her. Not again. Not ever.

"What if I moved back here? Would that make you happy?" he asked. Avery's head shot in his direction, and she stared at him with a look of disbelief.

"You'd do that? I mean, is that even an option?"

Was it an option? That was a good question. The rest of the band lived in LA, so practice would be difficult, but it could be done, couldn't it?

"Anything is possible. I don't have to stay in LA. Heck, I don't even have to stay in the band."

"What are you talking about?" She let out a half laugh. "Your band is your life. You're one of the biggest names of our time. You can't give that up. Not for me. I won't let you." She shook her head.

"What if I told you I'm tired of it?"

"I bet. It must be exhausting having raving fans all over the world, and all the money you could ever dream of for doing exactly what you love," she teased.

"Money isn't everything." He shot her a serious look. "And who says I still love it?"

"You're telling me you don't love making music?"

"Making music, yes. Touring, writing songs I'm forced to write, in a way that I'm being told to do it instead of the way I want to do it, that takes all the fun out of it for me. To be honest, it stopped being fun a long time ago."

"So, what do you want to do?"

"I don't know, but I do know one thing. I'm ready for a

change, and Arbor Shores might be just the change I'm looking for. It's been so good being back here. Being with you. Life is so simple here. I left town searching for happiness, but it was here waiting for me all along."

She scooted across the seat and slid next to him. He put his arm around her and pulled her close. "You're right, Shane. We don't have to figure this out today. Let's just forget I brought it up for now and see where this week takes us."

"Okay, but I meant what I said. We are going to make this work. I don't know how, or what that will even look like, but I know I'm never losing you again."

With those words, he felt Avery's head rest against his shoulder, and although she didn't say anything, he was sure they were on the same page for the first time in a long time. And that felt better than ever.

There was no way he would screw this up again.

Avery watched as Shane spent the afternoon painting the cabins, thinking of reasons to go check on him several times throughout the day. Her mom still hadn't returned, and she wasn't answering her cell phone, which was odd. Avery had plenty to keep her busy at the lodge, especially with the absence of her mother, who usually wrote checks for the deliveries that came in on Mondays, but by five, she was beat. It had been a long day, and she just wanted to go see Shane and let him know it was time to stop for the day.

She made her way down the hill in the golf cart, and was pleasantly surprised to find that some time throughout the hot afternoon, Shane had taken off his shirt. He was trimming the window on cabin number two in nothing but his blue jeans when she found him. She was actually surprised he hadn't drawn a crowd of guests from the resort. It was odd to find him alone and not being swarmed for autographs. Then again, that was a testament to how slow the resort actually was, although it was early week, and most of the weekend guests had already checked out.

"I brought you some lemonade," she said, walking up behind the ladder.

"And here I thought you were coming to help," he teased and gave her a grin before he took a big swig. "Thank you. This is exactly what I needed."

"Have dinner with me? It's the least I can do for all of your hard work. The cabins are looking great, by the way."

"Well, I barely finished two, but thank you."

"I really appreciate it. So, dinner?" She was wearing her heart on her sleeve, but she didn't care. As much as she hated the thought of him leaving, he was right. They could figure it out later. For now, she just wanted to enjoy herself and have some of the fun she'd been missing. She could feel herself coming around, and she was actually quite proud of herself for letting him back in.

"I'd love nothing more." He climbed down from the ladder. "I'll need to get a shower. Where would you like to go?"

"How about right here?"

"Huh?"

Avery walked to the back of the golf cart and retrieved a basket. He followed to see what she'd brought.

"I grabbed a couple of steaks and some sides from the kitchen. I figured we'd throw them on the grill at your cabin, and enjoy a summer evening by the lake."

"That sounds like a plan to me. What else have you got in there?" He playfully bumped her out of the way with his hip and started rummaging through the basket.

"Hey, you'll find out later." She tried to grab it back from him but it was too late. He was pulling the contents of the basket out and looking at what all she'd packed with an amused grin on his face.

"Marshmallows ... graham crackers ... chocolate ... red wine." He smiled at her, and she could feel her face reddening.

"If I didn't know better, I'd think you planned us a date night here in this basket."

She felt slightly foolish. Was it too much? "I just thought I'd give you the full experience. When was the last time you had s'mores or grilled out by the lake?"

He put the contents back in the bag and turned to face her, grabbing her hands. "Honestly, it's perfect. There's nothing I'd rather do than barbecue by the lake with you. I do have to shower though."

"Let's wrap up here. You can get a shower, and I'll start prepping."

She helped him pack up the painting supplies and put them on the porch of the cabin he'd been working on. Once back at Shane's cabin, he disappeared into the bathroom to shower, and she began shucking the corn and seasoning the steaks.

She heard the shower turn off, and he emerged in nothing but a tight white towel wrapped snug around his waist, his hair wet and tousled, looking like a tanned god with bulging abs.

"Those look great," he said eyeing the steaks, but she couldn't take her eyes off of him. "I'm going to go get dressed, and then I'll help," he said over his shoulder before disappearing into the bedroom.

Please get dressed. His rugged good looks were almost too much to take.

Shane emerged a few minutes later in gym shorts and a hoodie. He looked just as good in this getup as he had half-naked. What was happening inside of her? She hadn't had this reaction to a man in a long time. In fact, she hadn't had this reaction to a man since *him.*

Shane poured them both a glass of wine and led Avery by the hand out to the patio. "You relax." He placed her in a lounge chair and handed her a glass. "I'll light the grill."

She watched as he prepped the grill, and the comforting aroma of hot charcoal filled her nose with nostalgia. Her dad had always cooked on the grill, and that smell took her back every time. It was a smell she loved more than anything. She leaned back in her chair and took a sip of her wine, letting all the tension escape her body as she let out a long sigh. This was the first time she'd felt this relaxed in a long time, and there was nowhere else she'd rather be.

They ate dinner on a picnic table in front of the cabin, under the shade of a giant oak tree. The sun was getting low now, and she was getting a bit chilly, still in her sundress.

"How about I light a fire?" He motioned to the firepit.

"That'd be great." She got up and went into the cabin to get the fixings for the s'mores. She wandered into the bedroom and found his suitcase on the floor. She grabbed a sweatshirt out of his things. She used to love stealing his shirts back in the day. In fact, she still had his favorite U of M sweatshirt, but she'd never tell him that. It was soft and worn out from years of washes, and it was her favorite. There was no getting rid of it, even though the sleeves had begun to fray and there were a few holes and stains. She only wore it when home alone, and the holes and stains didn't bother Tipper much.

"I see you went shopping in my suitcase." He looked up at her and laughed, poking at the fire.

"I'll give it back."

"Yeah, right! I know how that goes." He smiled. "Keep it."

The sweatshirt had a hint of his scent and it comforted her. "If you insist," she agreed, shooting him a flirtatious grin.

They sat by the fire for several hours, talking about what they'd been doing over the years while they were apart. Shane played her a love song every now and then on his guitar, serenading her in the quiet summer night. It was dark now, and the sky was dusted with stars. The moon shone down on the lake, and the last few logs on the fire glowed before them, but it was slowly starting to go out. Shane tilted his head back and closed his eyes. He looked content, but there was something she needed to know before their evening came to an end. Something that had been on her mind for far too long.

"Man, it's so nice to be back. I sure do miss summers here. Thank you for a great day." He opened his eyes to look at her, and she met his eyes with a serious look.

She sat up straight in her chair, searching for the right words. "Shane, I need to know something."

He straightened his back and sat up to face her. "Anything."

"I need to know why you left the way you did." Her voice shook, but she had to know. They were so close back then; their love was real even if they were just kids. How could he just leave and never miss her or Arbor Shores? Not even once did he have a moment of weakness after he left. It didn't make sense.

"Take a walk with me down to the dock?" He stood up and held out his hand to her. She obliged, and they walked to the end of the dock in silence, the moon lighting the way.

They took a seat at the end of the dock and both dipped their feet into the water, which was surprisingly warm.

Shane rubbed at the back of his neck, and Avery could tell he was pausing to find the right words. He looked to be deep in thought, so she waited. This wasn't the time to push.

"Avery, there's something I never told you. Something I never told anyone. Something only the Knox family knows about, and still, it's never spoken of, even among us brothers."

"Go on," she said softly.

"You always knew my father was tough on us Knox boys, but I never told you just how tough."

She reached over and put her hand on his leg. She could see he was struggling.

"He was physical, Avery," he finally spat out the words. "In a violent way. Not just to our mother, but to me and the twins, mostly. Hunter was always his favorite, but he still got it, too, just not as bad. Probably because he tried harder to please him than the rest of us."

"I had no idea."

"There was nothing I ever did that pleased him. It seemed that no matter how hard I tried, he was never happy with my decisions. When I didn't make the football team my freshman year, you'd have thought the world was coming to an end. But I never wanted to play football. Football was Ethan's thing. Music was my thing." His jaw tightened. "And then, when I thought about going to college out of state, he exploded. He wanted me to go to Northern, and I couldn't bear to stay that close to home. It made me not want to go to college at all if that was my only option."

"So, that's why you never wanted to apply for college?"

"Things got worse as my parents were going through their divorce. Our home life was tumultuous, and he took it out on us boys. After graduation, I just wanted to get out of here. So did the twins. Heck, the only one who stayed in Arbor Shores was Hunter. I can't even imagine how he's dealt with Dad all these years."

"Why didn't you ever tell me?"

He scrubbed his face with his hand. "I was ashamed, I guess. I didn't want to burden you with my problems. Getting out of the house and being with you, being here at the resort with you and Dax and your family—which seemed perfect to me—that was the only time I was happy. It was an escape from the reality I was living at home, and when I was here with you, I didn't want to think about it. I just wanted to enjoy every moment."

Avery slid her body closer to him and put her arm around his waist. She rested her head on his shoulder, but didn't say a word, allowing him to continue.

"The night before I left, that was the worst it ever got. My mom had come back to the house to get the rest of her things. There was a bad fight, and I'd had enough. I stepped in to protect her, and he—"

"Shane, you don't have to say it."

"We called the cops, but of course, because of my father's power, that was never leaked, even in a small town like Arbor Shores. The next day, I was gone. Well, I was kicked out, so I had no choice but to leave. As long as I was leaving, I figured I might as well go as far away as possible. I'd always had a dream of making it in music, you know that. So, I left for California. I couldn't wait for you. You were still in your senior year."

"I wish you would've told me. I spent so many years wondering how you could just walk away from what we had. I never knew ..."

"I'm sorry I left you, Ave. I'm sorry I never came back. When I tell you it's the hardest thing I've ever done in my life, I mean it. But I had to get out of here and put Arbor Shores behind me. I had to or else I would've broken and come back to you, and I didn't want to be anywhere near him once I was old enough to make that decision. I had to be strong, and it was the first time in my life I was in control of my decisions and that felt good." He grabbed her hand and squeezed it. "But the leaving you part, that killed me. I just want you to know that." He turned to face her for the first time since he'd started talking, and she could see his eyes were moist with tears. She could tell he meant his words.

"I understand. I just wish you would've told me, that's all. You'll never know how much it hurt me when you left. You'll never know how many nights I cried myself to sleep wondering why you never thought about me or missed me, not even once." A hot tear escaped the corner of her eye.

"You weren't the only one who was hurting. And just so you know, there isn't a day that's gone by that I haven't thought about you. Still to this day. There isn't a song I've ever written that didn't have you in mind. They've all been for you."

"But why didn't you ever come back for me?"

"That part, I don't have an answer for. Maybe I was too ashamed to face you after I left you like I did. Call it being young, call it making bad decisions. Call it what you want. I call it the worst decision I've ever made."

"Well, in hindsight, as much as it hurt at the time, I'm glad I stayed here, or I wouldn't have had those last few years with my dad." The thought of not getting that time with her father filled her with emotion.

He stood up and held out his hands to pull her to her feet. She didn't need to hear another word, she was just grateful to finally know the truth.

She put her arms around his waist and nuzzled into his embrace, exhaling the last trace of doubt she had left in her.

It was as if nine years of heartache had finally been erased with one long overdue conversation.

CHAPTER 15

"There you are." Avery plopped her purse down on the chair across from her mother's desk and stood with a hand on her hip, ready for an explanation. "Where were you yesterday? I tried calling and texting you several times."

Meredith let out a long, exasperated sigh. "I went into the city to meet with the bank and then with our attorney." Her words had a somber tone, and Avery had a feeling bad news was coming.

"And?" Avery waited, afraid of what might come next.

"Well, the bank denied my request for an extension. So, I went to our lawyer to have him look over Hunter Knox's offer."

"What? Please tell me you did not accept the offer."

"I signed the papers, Avery."

"No, please tell me you didn't." Avery placed her hand on her forehead and circled around the office. "Didn't you get my note?"

"There's nothing we can do at this point to save the resort. We can't come up with what's needed in the next few weeks. We'd need a miracle."

"Mom, call the attorney and tell him you've changed your mind. We do not need to take Hunter's offer. Shane has offered to put on a concert here this weekend for the Jamboree. That's why I was trying to call you yesterday."

"You're telling me Shane Knox has agreed to host a concert at Arbor Shores Resort?"

"That's right. So, you can decline Hunter's offer because this will surely raise enough money."

"Well, let's think about this for a moment." Her mother began to pace. "Is his band flying in?"

Uh... Avery and Shane hadn't quite gotten that far yet. "I'm not exactly sure of the logistics, but he has agreed to headline the Jamboree, and we need to get the word out and start selling tickets as soon as possible."

"That's kind of him, Avery, but do we even have the capacity to house a rock star as big as Shane here at the resort? I mean, this could put us over code."

"Let's just figure out how much space we have, and we'll price tickets accordingly. Once at capacity, we'll sell out. Obviously, if we can get attendees to stay the weekend that would be ideal, so let's put together a concert and lodging deal for those coming from downstate."

"And how do you plan to get the word out on such short notice? We have less than a week."

"Simple. I called Channel 7 News this morning."

"You did what? We haven't even come up with a ticket price yet, or a way to sell the tickets. Or created an agreement for Shane, or—"

"Well, that's what we're doing now, Mom." Avery gave her mother a comforting smile, finally retreating to the chair. She pulled out her notepad. "Let's come up with our package price, and I'll put a link on our website. The story airs in a few hours so we have to get moving on this."

"You've really outdone yourself this time. It always amazes me how much you manage to get done before 9:00 a.m."

"Is it too late to decline Hunter's offer?"

"I don't know. I'll call the attorney's office and see what I can do." Meredith actually had a glimmer of hope on her face for the first time in a long time, and that made Avery happy. "So, you haven't mentioned yet why Shane has agreed to do this. Are the two of you rekindling old flames?"

Avery hesitated and took a deep breath. She hadn't thought about how she'd answer these types of questions. "We're just friends. Those flames died long ago." Avery didn't have it in her to answer questions about her and Shane just yet. Not until they figured out what they were doing themselves. For now, she was going to keep whatever was going on between her and Shane between them.

"Well, I just thought perhaps the two of you may have remembered how in love you once were."

"No, Mom, I don't have time for the complications of a relationship right now." There was no harm in telling her mom a little white lie just to buy herself time, right? Even if she was falling for Shane, it was too early in the morning to get into it. Plus, they had a concert to plan, and they were running out of time before the story aired.

Her and Shane's situation was complicated enough without everyone else's opinions. The last thing she needed was to have their relationship leaked to the media, and in a small town like Arbor Shores, news of her and Shane rekindling would travel fast. She saw the way his life was always plastered all over the tabloids. They'd have paparazzi all over the property if the media caught wind of Shane Knox being in a relationship. That would surely ruin the ambience of the resort and make the guests feel uncomfortable, and that's the last thing they needed while they were trying to rebuild the reputation of the resort. They needed to gain new business, not chase it away.

As much as she loved her mother and wanted to confide in someone, she knew her mom would be too excited, and the entire staff would know by day's end. For the sake of saving the resort, she'd have to keep this quiet. At least for now.

"Okay, okay. It just seems like a nice gesture from Shane.

He's obviously interested in you or he wouldn't still be here."
Her mother raised an eyebrow and gave her a pointed look.

The stress of getting everything finalized for the concert
before the story aired caused anxiety to ripple through Avery's
chest. She needed to nip this in the bud so her mom would stop
asking questions about her and Shane. Later, they could let her
know they were back together. But were they? It was too early to
know what would happen at the end of the week, even for her
and Shane.

"If he is interested in me, it's one sided. I refuse to let Hunter
Knox come in and tear down the resort. I'll do whatever I have
to do to raise the money to save the resort, and right now, if that
means playing nice with Shane, so be it." The words felt ice cold
as they left her lips, but she'd panicked. A wave of guilt hit her
for lying to her mother, but she'd have plenty of time later to tell
her mom the truth. First, she needed to get through this week and
the Jamboree. Then she'd know better what was going on
between her and Shane, and then they would make their
announcements. *Together.* That is, if they found a way to make a
relationship work, and *if* Shane decided to stay in Arbor Shores.

Shane entered the main lodge and was relieved to see there
wasn't anyone yet in the lobby, except for a hotel maid who was
making her way to the elevators. Finally, he'd be able to walk
through the lobby without being stopped for pictures and autographs. No sign of Avery, so he headed in the direction of the
office. As he drew closer, he could hear Avery and Meredith
talking with the door ajar. Avery's words hit him like a freight
train, head on.

"If he is interested in me, it's one sided. I refuse to let Hunter
Knox come in and tear down the resort. I'll do whatever I have
to do to raise the money to save the resort, and right now, if that
means playing nice with Shane, so be it."

Shane's heart slammed against his chest. Did he just hear her right? There was no denying it; he heard her words loud and clear. He needed to get outside before Avery came out of the office. He didn't want to see her. More importantly, he didn't want her to see the devastation on his face. Humiliation flooded through him. How could he be so foolish to think she was falling for him? It just didn't make sense. Avery wasn't the type to use someone. How could she feel this way after their night together? Why had he opened up to her about his past the way he had? Had she been playing him? Then again, it had been nine years since he'd known Avery. Maybe she had changed. This wasn't the Avery he thought he knew, or the one he thought he was falling in love with. Come to think of it, she didn't seem to start coming around until after he offered to put on the concert. Up until that point, she'd been standoffish. Now, it was all starting to make sense.

He hadn't felt this type of pain since the news of Naomi's affair went viral. Naomi hadn't had the decency to tell him herself, so he'd been blindsided when the tabloids published pictures of her in her co-star's arms. Shane had felt betrayed by her, and that's exactly the way he felt about Avery right now.

He couldn't get out of the lodge fast enough. He jogged down the hill, straight past his cabin, heading north up the shore. He didn't know where he was going; he just wanted to be as far away as possible. He jogged the shoreline until he couldn't catch his breath. He stopped and put his hands on his knees, trying to regain his composure. He kept walking for what seemed like an eternity. When he turned around to head back, the resort wasn't even in sight.

Finally, back at his cabin, he slammed the door behind him. He still felt the blow of Avery's words, and they stung as he played them over in his mind. How could he have misread their connection? Was she trying to get him back for breaking her heart long ago? Well, he wasn't going to be played for a fool. He knew what he had to do.

He pulled his cell phone off the coffee table where he'd powered it off yesterday. He hit the power button, and it began to light up like a Christmas tree. Thirty-seven missed calls between his manager and publicist. He started listening to the voicemails he'd missed.

Shane, you were expected in New York today. What happened?

Where are you? Why didn't you get on the jet? Call me.

Are you alive? Call me ASAP.

Shane Knox, you have some explaining to do.

He stopped listening after the first few. How could he be so foolish to blow off his career for Avery when she was just using him? He couldn't wrap his head around what was happening. His phone buzzed in his hand, startling him.

"Knox," he answered.

"Shane? I can't believe you answered. Where are you? Why didn't you get on the jet to New York?" James' high-pitched voice pierced his ear with question after question.

"Sorry, something came up."

"Something came up, Shane?" His manager's voice had risen even higher, and it was taking him back to a time reminiscent of his father's meltdowns. "And what is this I just heard about you putting on a concert in Michigan this weekend? You don't put on concerts without permission."

Man, good news travels fast. How could he possibly know that already? Avery's efforts to spread the word must be going better than she'd anticipated.

"I need permission to play music now?"

"Yes! You need permission from the label and you need a contract, and you don't play without your band. Remember your band? The tabloids are already calling Lori for the scoop. There's talk you are going solo. She's been on damage control all morning. What's going on, Shane? Talk to me."

"I'm not going solo. I'm back home, and I was going to sing a few songs at a Fourth of July party, that's all."

"A party? Doesn't look like a party to me. To me it looks like the biggest event the Midwest has ever seen."

"How do you even know about it?"

"Why? Were you trying to hide it from me? I'd like to remind you that you are scheduled for *The Aftershow* on Saturday. Did you forget about that, too, like you forgot to get on the plane? You blow off this opportunity, and the label is going to drop you." Drop him? For missing one appearance? He had a feeling his manager was trying to strong-arm him, but was it worth the chance of ending his career? "Lori had several appearances lined up for you yesterday and today. This doesn't look good for you, Shane."

"Get me a jet. I'll be at the airport in one hour." He smashed the power button and shoved his phone into his pocket. He wasn't ready to deal with the aftermath of his decisions. How could he have been so blinded by Avery? His hurt was growing into anger now. It was time to pack and leave Arbor Shores, once and for all. Now his only problem was how to get out of here before Avery showed up. To think he'd thought he'd found love again. He had been ready to stay here and make a new life with Avery. He thought she wanted the same. How could he have misinterpreted her feelings for him?

He moved quickly around the cabin, gathering his things and throwing his stuff into his suitcase. He took one final look around to make sure he had everything, and then walked out to the rental car, pleased to find that there wasn't anyone around except a couple sitting out on their porch drinking coffee a few cabins down, but they didn't seem to notice him. He threw his suitcase in the trunk and hightailed it out of the side entrance by the golf course, being careful not to go anywhere near the main lodge. The last thing he wanted to do was see Avery. As he went through the gates and turned onto the main road that led to the city, he knew this was the last time he'd be leaving Arbor Shores.

This time, he was leaving for good.

CHAPTER 16

*A*very's morning had been busy, and time had gotten away from her. She and Meredith came up with a killer concert and lodging package, and once the news aired the story, the phones were ringing off the hook. Their website couldn't handle the traffic, and the server had quickly crashed, leaving Avery, Meredith and the front desk receptionist to take all reservations and ticket sales by phone. They had sold out in less than two hours, and Avery was beyond pleased with the results. She couldn't wait to tell Shane.

"Mom, I'm heading down to take Shane some lunch," she said, poking her head into the office.

"Good job today, Avery. This really was a great idea. I've been punching the numbers and we should have more than we need to pay the bank when all is said and done."

"Did you hear from the attorney?"

"Yes, he hadn't sent the acceptance letter yet. I asked him to buy us some time. If this goes off the way we are planning, we'll be able to decline the offer."

"Decline it, Mom. This is happening. The resort is already booked to capacity, and the concert is sold out."

"Hey, Avery? Make sure you send Shane my love, and give him a big hug from me. This is really great of him to do."

"Will do," she said, before hurrying down the hallway.

It was early afternoon now, and Avery figured Shane was probably getting hungry from painting. She couldn't wait to tell him the news. She couldn't stop thinking about their day together yesterday and how much she'd enjoyed their evening by the lake. Him opening up about his past had brought them closer together, to a level they'd never experienced before. She was starting to feel like they could make this work somehow, no matter what that looked like. They would figure that part out. All she knew is that she was sure she didn't want to lose him ever again. She hadn't had butterflies like this in years. In fact, she hadn't had butterflies like this since they were teenagers.

She reached the shore and headed straight to cabin number two. No sign of Shane. That's odd. She circled the cabin in the golf cart just to be certain, but the supplies were in the exact place where they had left them on the cabin porch the night before. Something twisted in her stomach. Something wasn't right.

She pushed the gas pedal to the floor but the golf cart didn't pick up any additional speed as it made its way down the path. She reached Shane's cabin and hopped out of the cart, leaving his lunch on the seat. The only thing on her mind was finding out where he was. Was he sick? She hadn't heard from him, but then again, they hadn't even bothered to exchange numbers, so how would she know? Her heart sank as thoughts of Shane lying alone in his cabin, sick or hurt, danced through her mind. She reached the cabin door and knocked hard, pausing to listen for footsteps. Nothing. She knocked again, pressing her ear to the door. No sign of movement inside. She turned the handle and pushed the door open.

Nothing could prepare her for the disappointment that assaulted her when she walked inside.

The cabin was empty. No sign of Shane, and no sign of his

belongings. She went straight to the bedroom; just a ball of sheets on the bed—no suitcase, no dirty clothes sprinkled around the room like the night before. She went to his bathroom, no toiletries. Everything was gone. There was absolutely no sign of Shane anywhere.

It was a kick to the gut, one that knocked the wind right out of her. Hot tears welled up in her eyes as she searched every inch of the cabin for a note or an explanation. But nothing.

Shane Knox was gone.

She hadn't felt this pain, this abandonment, since the first time he'd left. At least back then, he had left her a note. A note that she still kept in a shoebox at the top of her bedroom closet along with a dried corsage he'd given her on his prom night. Granted, the note was only a few lines:

Ave,

I had to leave and follow my dreams. I hope you will do the same. No time to explain, but I'll come back for you someday. Promise. Wait for me.

Love you always,

Shane

That note had hurt. It killed her, but at least he'd had the decency to tell her he was leaving. Where was the note this time? Not having an explanation hurt even worse. She curled into a ball on his bed. His scent still lingered on his pillow, filling her nose and her heart with sadness. The hollowness in her chest was a constant reminder of the pain she was now left with. She cried and she cried until there were no more tears left in her. How could she have been so foolish as to let this man back into her life? What about the concert? What about the half-painted cabins? She was left with a mess, and she didn't have the slightest idea where to begin. They'd just sold out the entire resort for the concert that Shane was set to headline. Now they'd have to cancel and refund everyone. Now, they'd have to accept Hunter's offer, and they'd lose Arbor Shores Resort once and for all.

But those thoughts paled in comparison to the pain his leaving left inside of her. It was the knowing that she'd lost him once again that was at the forefront of her mind. The sorrow in her heart was like nothing she'd ever felt. It just didn't make sense. Why would he do this?

It really had been too good to be true.

After a good hour of lying on the bed, unable to move, she finally peeled herself up and walked to the bathroom to splash water on her face. It was time to pull herself together and think of her next steps. Shane may have left her once again, but she didn't have time to deal with the heartache. Right now, she had to figure out a way to get the cabins finished and find someone new to headline the event. The event had to go on. She was determined to find a way to fix this, and she knew she couldn't tell her mother Shane had left. She'd just keep that to herself for now until she figured everything out.

She made her way over to cabin number two and popped open the paint, pouring it into the drop pan. She picked up the paint roller and headed to the spot where Shane had left off the day before. She painted and thought, and painted and thought, until the cabin was finished and it was on to the next. She still hadn't come up with a single idea of how she was going to pull off the Jamboree without Shane. Mostly, her thoughts were flooded with memories of the day before, and the puzzle she was trying to put together in her mind. How she had misinterpreted his affection was mind boggling.

Shane reached the airport in record time and whipped his car into the rental agency that was conveniently located at the airport, not off site like some of the bigger ones. That was one thing he'd miss about this place—the simplicity of everything. The other thing he'd miss was Avery.

He'd spent the drive into the city playing her words over

and over in his mind. How could he have been so foolish? How had he misread her feelings for him? Up until that moment, he was sure he would have Avery back forever. He was ready to move his life back to Arbor Shores as home base. He was already envisioning what their life would look like. They would run the resort together and he'd help her turn it green. He would fly to LA as needed to practice with the band, or the band would fly out to him. If he went on tour, Avery could fly to different cities to meet up with him. That is, if he decided to continue to tour and make music. He wasn't quite sure that's what he still wanted. At this point, all he wanted was to start over with Avery in Arbor Shores where he belonged. Or so he thought.

The loss he felt was far worse than any heartache he'd ever experienced. Naomi Wilde's affair didn't hold a candle to this pain. The only thing he was sure of is that he would never open his heart up again. Not ever.

Shane's phone buzzed and he expected it to be his manager. *Man, what now?* He was getting on the plane. He didn't feel like another lecture, so he ignored the buzzing in his pocket as he made his way to the jet. The buzzing continued, over and over, until he finally pulled the phone out of his back pocket.

A text from Hunter? What did his brother want? He never heard from Hunter, so he could only assume he was calling because word of the concert was likely spreading like wildfire. *Oh man, the concert.* A pang of guilt pulsed through him for leaving Avery and Meredith with no one to headline their Jamboree. They would surely lose the resort now, and Shane would have to deal with the press mess that would come from no-showing the event, but he had no choice. He couldn't let Avery use him.

Another text came in from Hunter. Curiosity finally got the best from him, so he clicked on his name to read it:

Call me ASAP. It's Dad.

Shane had just reached the stairs to the jet.

"I'm sorry, I need a minute," he told the private attendant who was waiting to greet him.

He walked away from the roar of the engines and called Hunter. "Hey, it's Shane. What happened?"

All he could hear was heavy breathing on the other end and sniffling that hinted at tears, and he was sure something was not right. Hunter was trying to speak, but he was choked up, and Shane knew something bad had happened.

"Hunter, talk to me, bro. What happened?"

"It's Dad," Hunter finally got the words out through shaky breath.

"What do you mean? What happened, Hunter?" Shane's voice was stern. Instantly, the lifelong feud between him and his brother meant nothing. His brother was hurting, and something had happened to their father. He was sure of it.

"Dad had a heart attack, Shane," he bellowed into the receiver. "The ambulance just took him. I'm with Valerie, and we're on our way to the hospital."

"Is he going to be okay?" Shane raised his voice, trying to get his younger brother to gain composure and talk.

"I don't know."

"Which hospital?"

"Traverse General."

"I'll be right there."

~

The next several hours were a blur; a complete whirlwind. Shane arrived at the hospital to find Hunter and Valerie in the waiting room, both in tears.

When the doctor finally came out to share the news, they were told that Carter had survived but would need a triple bypass. They were all relieved that the doctors were able to save him, but he wasn't in the clear just yet as he still needed major surgery.

They were able to track down one of the twins, Ethan, who played pro football but hadn't started summer training yet. He was at home in Green Bay and was headed out on the next available flight. But they weren't able to track down the other twin, Chase, the drifter of the Knox brothers. Chase was the wild child, the bad boy, who unlike Shane, Ethan, and Hunter, could never quite find his groove of what he wanted to do with his life, so he mostly traveled, never settling to put down permanent roots anywhere. His cell phone was turned off and went straight to voicemail. They'd left several messages, but they'd yet to be returned.

Shane was just glad he hadn't gotten on that jet to New York. Hunter and Valerie needed him and it felt good that he could be there for them. He didn't feel great about the way things had ended between him and his father the other night, and it was putting things into perspective about what was really important in life. Even though his father was tough on him and his brothers growing up, he was still their dad, and Shane didn't want to see anything bad happen to him. He wasn't quite ready to have a relationship with him, but he wanted to make sure he'd be okay before he left Arbor Shores again. If nothing else, at least for Hunter's sake, who wasn't taking it well.

The surgery was a success, but Carter would need to stay in the hospital and recover. Valerie wouldn't leave Carter's bedside, and it was showing Shane a different side of her that he'd never seen before. She really did love his father. Perhaps he'd misjudged her all these years.

Hunter and Shane went back to the Knox estate to shower and rest. Valerie had insisted the two boys go and wait for Ethan. Shane grabbed two beers out of the fridge and found Hunter sitting on the back veranda. He twisted off the caps, handed one to Hunter, and took a chair beside him. They both sat in silence for a bit. Shane could only assume Hunter was as mentally and emotionally drained as he was.

"Shane," Hunter said, finally breaking the silence. "I want

you to know…" His voice trailed off as he struggled to find the words. "I just wanted to say I'm glad you're here."

"Listen, Hunter." Shane put his beer down and pushed both hands through his hair, struggling to find his own words. Verbal communication between the Knoxes had never been their strong suit. Growing up in this house, they were taught against it, so it was no wonder both boys were struggling to say what was on their mind. "I'm sorry I haven't been around. You know I had my reasons, but none of that really matters right now. But I'm here now, and even though we haven't always been close, you're my brother and I want to make things right between us."

"I'd like that." Hunter looked over at Shane and gave him a small smile, likely the most he could muster up. "Hey, I almost forgot with everything that's been going on that you have the concert at the resort on Saturday."

Shane didn't even want to think about it, much less talk about it. He'd made the decision that he wasn't going to put on the concert but he still hadn't told anyone.

"You know, I was pretty upset when Meredith turned down my offer," Hunter admitted. "But all of that seems so trivial now."

"Wait, Meredith turned it down?"

"Yep. Apparently, your concert sold out in less than two hours, and they filled not only the venue to capacity, but each room and cabin in the resort. You saved their resort, Shane. You must really love that girl."

Shane felt like someone had reached into his chest, squeezed, and then twisted. He didn't even know the concert had sold out. How could he? He'd left before speaking with Avery. A wave of guilt washed over him as he envisioned Avery and Meredith cancelling and refunding a full venue. They'd surely lose the resort now, and they'd already declined Hunter's offer. With all that was going on with their father, Hunter wouldn't likely be interested in it now. What would they do? The bank would probably foreclose or they'd have to take a lowball offer from a developer.

No, he refused to take on this guilt. He'd already made up his mind. He wasn't doing the concert. He'd heard Avery. She was playing with his emotions so she could use him to save the resort. She didn't care about him. Somewhere down the line she became heartless, just like Naomi. It just didn't add up. That's not the Avery he knew and not the one he thought he was falling back in love with.

"So, are you?" Hunter asked, knocking him from his thoughts.

"Huh?"

"Are you in love with Avery?"

Shane tilted his head back and looked up at the sky, as if the answer to that very question was going to rain down upon him.

"Honestly, I thought I was falling for her again."

"You thought?"

"Yeah."

"And now?"

Shane paused and let out a long sigh. "Now, I'm thinking I don't even know that girl anymore."

"That's too bad. You two really had something special once upon a time."

"We were kids. People change."

Avery had changed.

CHAPTER 17

*W*ord of Carter's heart attack spread rapidly through Arbor Shores, yet Avery was one of the last to find out since she had thrown herself into the project of finishing the cabins and had shut off all communication with the outside world.

"Avery Grace, I've been looking all over for you," Meredith said, approaching the ladder Avery was standing on.

"I've been down here."

"Have you stopped answering your phone?"

"I powered it off. What's up?" She never skipped a beat and continued painting the trim. She'd been hoping she wouldn't have to see her mother again today. She still hadn't figured out what to tell her.

"I figured you were with Shane. How's he holding up?"

"How's *he* holding up?" She nearly dropped her paintbrush as she paused to stare at her mother in disbelief.

"He must be with Hunter. I've already sent flowers from us. I feel terrible for those boys. Any news on Carter?"

"Mom, what are you talking about?" Avery climbed down the ladder to meet her mother face-to-face.

"Carter Knox suffered a massive heart attack, Avery. How is it possible you haven't heard? Haven't you talked to Shane?"

"What? No! I hadn't heard. Shane's not here and I just figured ..." Ah, so now it all made sense. No wonder Shane had disappeared. He must've left to be with his family. Her heart sank to her stomach. How could she have been so foolish? Here she was drowning in her sorrows thinking Shane had abandoned her, when really, he'd been dealing with a family crisis across town. She had to get to him.

"Mom, I have to go find Shane."

"Yes, go be with him, dear. He needs you now more than ever."

Avery got in her car and headed toward Lakeview Estates. She felt a variety of emotions ranging from sadness for the Knox family, to even a bit of relief that she had misread the situation with Shane, and that he hadn't left her after all. She'd had no idea that he was still in Arbor Shores. She'd been sure he was back in California by now, never to be heard from again. Now, she couldn't help but feel massive guilt for the way she'd assumed he'd left, and for how she'd shut herself off from the world.

She pulled her car into Lakeview Estates and was met by the guard. News vans were lined on each side of the road, unable to enter. She wondered how she'd ever get through.

"Address and name, young lady?" the stout guard asked.

"Knox estate. I'm Avery Cooke."

"Hold tight." He disappeared into the shack and came back a few minutes later.

"Well, you must be family because you're the only one who's been permitted access all day. Sorry to hear about Carter. He's a good man." He nodded and then lifted the gate to let her through. A good man? Avery didn't know if she'd go that far.

She couldn't help but remember what Shane had told her on the dock. Regardless, he was still Shane's father. She couldn't bear to think of what Shane must be feeling, having been gone from the family for so long. She hoped he wasn't beating himself up with guilt.

She reached the front of the house, and Hunter met her at the door.

"Hunter, I'm so sorry to hear about your father." She leaned in and hugged him, not knowing how he would respond considering their run-in at Ripples on Sunday. He embraced her and accepted it in a way that told her he'd needed it.

"Thank you, Avery. I buzzed you in, but Shane doesn't know you're here. He's on a call with his publicist at the moment."

"Oh, well, thank you. I thought I'd better come see how he's doing. How both of you are doing, that is."

"As good as can be expected, I suppose." He held open the door, and she went inside. "You'll find Shane out back on the veranda. I'll give you two some privacy."

"Thank you."

"Hey, Avery?" Hunter called out to her as she made her way through the foyer.

"Yes?" She turned back to face him.

"I just wanted to say I'm sorry for what I said to you the other day."

"It's okay, Hunter. There was truth to your words."

"No, there wasn't. I was just being hurtful. You do a nice job with the resort. Your father would be proud." He gave her a sincere smile and looked down at his feet. What had come over him? This was the real Hunter she remembered, before he'd gotten into the business world. Maybe Carter's heart attack had reminded him of what was important. Either way, she'd needed to hear that, and she was grateful for his words.

"Thank you. That means more to me than you'll ever know." She returned the smile and then made her way through the massive living area, and out the French doors off the backside of the house. It was surreal being back here. She hadn't been in the Knox residence since she was a teenager, though it had changed quite a bit since then. She suspected that Valerie had redecorated after she moved in.

She cleared her throat and Shane turned, with his phone to his ear. "I have to go. I'll call you back," he said into the receiver and then tossed his cell onto the patio table. He crossed his arms over his chest and waited for Avery to speak.

Not knowing what to say, she quickly went to him and threw her arms around him. "I'm so sorry to hear about your father. I came as soon as I heard."

"Why are you here, Avery?" His stance was stiff; he didn't return her embrace.

She stepped back. "I-I just thought … I wanted to be here for you if you need me."

"Why do you care what I need?"

Why was he being so cold? This wasn't the same Shane that she'd been spending time with.

"Because I care about you." She stepped forward and reached out her hand to place it on his arm, but he stepped back to avoid the contact.

"Don't act like you care about me, Avery. This isn't the time for games. I'm dealing with a lot here if you can't tell. In fact, you should probably leave."

She couldn't believe his words. This was not at all what she'd expected; she wasn't prepared to be pushed away. A lump formed in her throat. Maybe he was just eaten up with guilt. After losing her own father, she knew firsthand how hard a day like this must be on him. She was willing to cut him some slack, even if it wasn't adding up.

"Okay, I'll go. But please know that I'm here for you if you need me." She turned to walk away, tears threatening to spill from her eyes. Her feelings were hurt, but she would give him his space. She stopped and turned back to ask, "Can I at least leave you my number in case you need anything?"

"You know, Avery, I don't think that will be necessary."

What was going on? Was this the same man she thought she was falling for?

"Did I do something to upset you?" she asked. She wasn't leaving without an explanation.

"I know you're just using me to save your resort. You played me for a fool."

"What are you talking about?" She moved toward him and stood before him with both hands on her hips. How dare he accuse her of such a thing.

"I heard you and your mom, Avery. I heard you say you were just playing nice because you'd do anything to save the resort."

"What? No! You have it all wrong." How could he have heard that conversation? She was in the office, alone with her mother. Panic raced through her chest. Why had she said that to her mom in the first place? How would she ever make Shane understand she hadn't meant a word of it?

"I heard you with my own two ears. I was coming to find you in the office when I heard you tell your mom that you have absolutely no interest in me. So please, don't come here and act like you care for me. This isn't the time."

"Shane, I just said that to my mom because I wasn't prepared to answer questions about us, and I didn't have time for her meddling." She stepped even closer to him now, placing her hand on his arm. "You have to believe me."

A long silence fell between them. "I don't know what to believe." He turned to face the woods. She placed her arms around his waist and laid her head on his back, embracing him in a final attempt to let him know her true feelings.

"You don't have to believe me, but I'm telling you the truth. The truth is, I love you, Shane. I never stopped loving you, but I wasn't ready to have that conversation with anyone. I wasn't even ready to have it with myself. But after I found you gone, I thought you'd left me again. It hurt even worse than the first time. I thought for sure I'd never see you again. That's when I knew I was one hundred percent head over heels in love with you."

He turned to face her. His brow had softened. Did he believe her?

"Well, I did leave. You were right. I was at the airport when I received the call from Hunter."

Now it was her turn to retreat. He had left her again, after all? "So, you did leave without saying goodbye?"

"After I heard what you said, I just wanted to be as far away from Arbor Shores as possible."

Anger rose to the surface. Avery willed herself to calm down, but the words kept coming out. "Over a misunderstanding? Is that what you do every time something doesn't go right in your life? You flee? You don't even stick around to find out what's going on, you just take off?"

"Your words hurt me, Avery. I was falling for you, too." His voice was rough and lacking emotion. Could she trust him? Did she want to give him a shot again if every time they argued, he might leave her again?

"You can't keep running away, Shane. You have to face things head-on. And you have to trust that when you do, I'll be standing beside you. Or else, this isn't going to work. I can't deal with you leaving every time you get upset. I would always worry about you leaving me."

"So, what are you saying?"

"I'm saying that you're either in wholeheartedly, or you're out. I can't take this back-and-forth."

"I can't deal with this right now. This isn't the time for this conversation. I have to think about all of this. I'm still really hurt by what I heard. I need some time."

Time was something they didn't have much of, especially with the concert looming. She didn't want to ask, not at a time like this, but she had to know. "I assume the concert is cancelled considering all that's going on?"

Silence fell between them. Shane rubbed at the back of his

neck. "I don't know," he finally said. A look of frustration washed over his face.

"I'll tell you what." Avery took a step closer and lowered her voice. "If you need to cancel due to what's going on with your dad, I'll understand. But if you leave and I don't hear from you, I'll know what I mean to you once and for all." She headed toward the slider and turned to face him one last time. "I came here to offer my support. I'm genuinely sorry about your father. If you need me, you know where to find me."

She headed in the house, through the Knox residence, and back to her car, where she finally let the tears that had been welling in her eyes fall.

Ethan arrived from the airport, and all three brothers headed up to the hospital the following morning. Carter was in recovery now, so they would be able to go in and see him for the first time since the heart attack.

When they arrived at the hospital, the brothers gathered in the waiting room as they waited for Valerie to come out and get them. They were catching up from years of being apart, and Shane was thrilled to be with his brothers, even if the circumstances were less than desirable.

But Avery's words still rang in his ears. Would he really run every time something didn't go his way? Is that what she thought of him? And, more importantly, was it true? That's what scared him the most. He had been ready to hightail it out of Arbor Shores when he'd heard Avery's conversation with Meredith. And he was able to leave her once, even though it haunted him for the entire nine years he was gone.

With the concert right around the corner, Shane had a decision to make. If Avery was telling the truth, then he felt like a fool for leaving her again. But was she telling the truth? She'd sounded so convincing when she spoke those words to her mother. Her words were ice cold, her voice without emotion. He had played it over and over in his mind, and each time he did, it made him want to retreat even more. He was finding it too hard to accept that there was no truth to her words. With all that was going on, his head was spinning and he didn't know what to believe.

If he didn't show up to the concert, he would be saying goodbye to Avery forever. And if he did show up, he was showing her he still loved her enough to stick around, and he'd prove her wrong. This was his final chance to win her back, if that's even what he truly wanted. But now he wasn't sure. He wished there was some way to find the answer. To know the truth.

"Ethan, I'm so glad you could be here," Valerie said as she opened the door to the waiting room. His brother got up and met her with a warm embrace. If one good thing was coming from this tragedy, it was bringing the Knox brothers back together again. Shane wanted to have a relationship with his brothers, it's just that they all had busy lives and were spread across the US. They didn't keep in touch as much as they should. But had Shane even tried to keep in touch? He was guilty of not making the effort on his end, but all of that was going to change. He was beginning to see the error of his ways and he was ready to accept responsibility for falling out with his family.

Perhaps he had been a bit selfish all these years.

For the first time in his life, Shane saw his father in a different light. Restricted to the hospital bed with tubes and monitors hooked up to him, Carter had a look of vulnerability about him that Shane had never witnessed.

The boys gathered around the bedside, and Valerie excused herself to go get some coffee. Shane suspected she just wanted to give the boys some privacy with their father.

"I can't believe I have three of you boys in one room." Carter's voice was weak.

"Glad to be here, Dad. We're just happy you're going to be okay," Ethan said, reaching down to put his hand on his father's arm.

"Of course I'll be okay. I'm a Knox." There it was—that tough spirit his father always carried. Shane could appreciate those words, and in that moment, he was proud to be a Knox, too. Perhaps for the first time in his life.

"I want to tell you all something while I have you here," his father spoke slowly. "I know I wasn't always easy on you boys, but that's just because I was trying to make you tough." He coughed and the machine beeped. He looked tired, as if getting the words out was taking all of his energy.

"We know that, Dad," Shane reassured him. "You don't need to say anything more." But did he? Shane still had resentment toward his father for just how tough he was on them, but he was willing to hear him out. This wasn't the time or the place for rebuttal. Perhaps this was a time for forgiveness.

"No, I need to say this." He took a deep breath and paused before continuing. "This puts things in perspective, lying here, helpless, depending on others to take care of you. I didn't want you boys to ever have to depend on anyone." He paused again to catch his breath. "And look at you now. I'm proud of you boys. I'm proud of the men you've become."

Shane knew his father may never actually say the words he needed to hear, that he was sorry for the pain he had inflicted, but he took this as the best apology Carter could give in this moment, and it was a start in the right direction. Shane would never be close with his dad, but he could appreciate that his father was beginning to see the error in his ways. He'd never once been told in his life that his father was proud of him, and those words meant more than anyone would ever know.

Carter's eyes began to close. It was clear those words had taken every ounce of energy he had.

"Get some rest, Dad," Shane said, and squeezed his father's hand. Carter opened his eyes and looked at him and nodded before closing them again, and that's all Shane needed. He knew his time with his father was complete.

The three Knox brothers spent the next forty-eight hours getting reacquainted and keeping Valerie in good spirits. After their final hospital visit on Friday, they learned that their father would be released, and Valerie was preparing to bring him home. With a long week behind them, they headed for Ripples to grab something to eat. Shane was looking forward to spending one last evening with his brothers before Ethan left town again, and he hoped they would keep in touch moving forward. It was just too bad Chase wasn't there to join them.

Hunter pulled his Range Rover into the parking lot, which was packed, and the boys headed toward the entrance. It was Friday night, and music spilled out from the patio. Shane's phone buzzed. He pulled it from his pocket.

"You guys go on in; I have to take this. I'll meet you inside." He walked toward the road to move away from the noise. "Knox."

"Shane, James here. How's your father?" He could tell his manager was trying to be polite, an unnatural act for him.

"He's recovering. What do you need, James?"

"I just wanted to remind you that you're still expected at the The *Aftershow* tomorrow. Now, Lori got you out of all the appearances she had set up in New York this week due to a family emergency, but it's time to get back to your life. The band needs you. Distant Union needs this appearance to get back in the good graces with the label."

"I'm not sure if you remember, but my father had a heart attack."

"I know, but you just said he's recovering, and life goes on. The show must go on."

"Perhaps you could give me some space to be with my family before you start harassing me about this?"

"I'm not harassing you, Shane. This is your career on the line. It's my job to make sure you don't screw it up. Now, I've seen the news that you've sold out a venue for tomorrow. The label has found out about it, and they are not happy. They're saying it's a breach of contract if you put on that concert."

"A breach of contract? To put on a concert in my hometown?"

"That's right. Read your contract."

"And if I don't go to New York tomorrow?"

"I'll put it to you this way, to be very clear. You either get on the plane and make the *The Aftershow* appearance tomorrow, or the label is going to drop you."

"Drop me? I'm the lead singer!"

"Everyone is replaceable, Shane. Now, I expect you to be at the airport tomorrow. I've emailed your itinerary. Don't screw this up." The line went dead. Shane couldn't believe the audacity of his manager. Who calls someone about business when their father is laid up in the hospital? The thought was making his blood boil. He didn't even know at this point if he wanted to continue his career. He'd spent the last nine years traveling with his band, different hotel rooms every night. Same song, different day. Maybe it was time for a change. Yet, he didn't want to let his band down, or his fans—the two things he truly loved about his career. Wasn't there some way to have it all?

Right now, he wasn't going to think about it. The only thing he wanted to think about was catching up with his brothers. Something that should have happened long ago.

He'd make his final decision in the morning.

CHAPTER 18

*A*very woke early, after a night of fitful sleep. She'd tossed and turned all night thinking about Shane's words, and worrying about the concert. If he didn't show, that would be the end of Arbor Shores Resort. She'd have to refund all those people, and not only would that ruin the reputation of the resort, but they wouldn't be able to pay the bank the money they owed to save it. And if he didn't show, that would also mean the end of Shane and Avery forever. She wasn't quite sure which was bothering her more.

Despite her dismal mood, she dressed in her Independence Day outfit—white shorts and a blue tank top adorned with white stars. She had made plans to meet Rylee to watch the first half of the parade, then she'd have to race to the resort to beat the crowd.

She arrived in town and parked her car behind NovelTea Books and Teahouse. The owner, Emma, was a good friend, and she knew she could park there anytime. From there, it was just a short walk to Main Street where families dressed in red, white, and blue were all lined up along the street. She normally loved this holiday; it always started with a parade, followed by a barbecue at the resort, and then fireworks at night over the lake.

But this year, her thoughts were consumed with the concert, and with Shane. The fate of the resort rested in his hands. She had no idea whether he'd show or not.

She located Rylee on the other side of Main Street. Rylee was waving her down, so she headed over. "Hey." Avery plastered a smile on her face and leaned in for a hug. "Happy Fourth."

"Uh-oh, what's wrong?" Rylee asked, a concerned look on her face as she studied Avery.

"What do you mean?"

"You're my best friend. I can tell when something's wrong." Rylee took off her sunglasses.

"I'm just worried about today."

"What are you worried about? It's all going to go off without a hitch."

"I'm worried Shane might not show for the concert."

"Well, of course he will. Why wouldn't he?"

"So much has happened this week, Ry. I think I've really screwed things up this time." Avery held her hand over her eyes to shade the sun as she scanned the crowd for Shane to see if he might be there. He'd always loved this parade. No sign of him. Of course, he couldn't be around; this crowd would swarm him. But still, she had to hope.

"I don't know what happened, but I know this much. That man is crazy about you. He'll be there."

"I'm not so sure." She looked at her friend who was studying her face.

"Come on, I can tell you're not into this. Let's get going to the resort. I'll help you with last minute stuff before my shift starts at Ripples. I know it's going to be a great day, and Shane will be there."

Avery wanted to believe her friend, but she just wasn't sure. She waited for an opening between floats and then darted across the street and back to her car. She was going to get the concert set up and hope for the best. If Shane didn't show, she would deal with the repercussions when the time came. Right now, she was going to try to remain positive.

She walked into the lodge to find a full lobby and a line at check in. There was a buzz in the room, and she kept hearing Shane's name as she made her way through the crowd. *This will be a disaster if he doesn't show.* Still, all she could do was try to remain positive.

"Good morning, dear. Happy Fourth," her mother greeted her when she made her way out onto the terrace. She could see the stage had been set up on the golf course, at the end of the first green, and she wondered how hole one would fare after the concert. Oh well, repairing a green was a small price to pay.

"What time will Shane be arriving? He needs to do a sound check with the AV crew."

She wasn't about to tell her mother that he may not be coming. Meredith was in far too good of a mood to kill her spirits, and telling her wouldn't change the outcome of whether Shane showed or not, so Avery's plan was to keep quiet and hope for the best. "I'll go check the stage. Do you need me for anything up here?"

"We have it covered. Registration has been a mess, but we're getting through it. Avery, I just want to say, this is the best idea you've had yet. You really saved the resort."

Avery gave her mother a half smile and walked toward the golf course. Worry had her stomach twisted in knots. She watched as people lined up at the outdoor bar as patriotic music floated through the speakers. It was two hours until showtime, and no sign of Shane as of yet.

"Hey, Jordan. Shane here by any chance?" she asked one of the hotel bellhops who was sitting in as a stagehand for the day.

"I was hoping he'd be with you. We need to get this sound check in. Can you tell him to hurry before people start claiming space on the lawn?"

"I'll get on that." She didn't have a way to contact Shane

even if she wanted to. All she could do was wait with bated breath.

Jordan disappeared in the back, and she was grateful for it. She needed to be alone and collect her thoughts. What would she do if he didn't show?

The next hour went by quickly as Avery and Rylee helped Meredith back at the lodge. The patio was full now, and the outdoor bars that had been set up were running out of ice, beer and wine. The hot dog stands set up around the property ran through their first cases of dogs in a hurry, and the three of them scrambled to keep everything stocked. They were at full capacity now, and Avery noticed the stretch of green in front of the stage was filled with lawn chairs and blankets. Not a patch of grass in sight. But still, no sign of Shane.

With the show set to begin at two o'clock, it was now quarter to two and he hadn't arrived. It was fair to assume at this point he wasn't coming, so now she needed to do what she'd been hoping to avoid. First, she'd have to tell her mother, and then she'd have to make an announcement to all the guests who had paid good money to stay at the resort and hear Shane's concert.

"Look at this place, Avery." Her mother put an arm around her shoulders and gave her a squeeze. "I don't think I've ever seen this place filled to capacity, even when your father was alive. He'd be proud of you, dear."

"Mom, there's something I have to tell you."

"Can it wait? I need to get out to the stage before the show starts. I want to make sure Shane has everything he needs. Plus, I haven't had a chance to offer my support regarding Carter."

"Well, that's the thing, Mom." She took a deep breath. "Shane isn't here."

"What? What on earth do you mean? Did something happen to him? Is he okay?"

"He's fine, Mom. He just didn't show."

"Well, he can't just not show. He's scheduled to put on a concert for all of these people. He would never just not show."

"Think again, because that's exactly what he did."

Meredith looked out at the golf course covered in people and raised up onto her tiptoes as if she'd be able to locate him.

"Please tell me this is a joke. What will we tell all these people? We will have a riot if we have to announce that Shane isn't here. Did you two get into a fight? Why would he not come, Avery?"

Her mild-tempered mother, who rarely lost her cool, was now firing questions at her left and right. Avery's head was beginning to throb. She didn't know how to answer her mother or what to do about the situation. That confusion was only part of the emotions that were swirling inside her. The fact that Shane didn't show meant she and Shane were over, forever.

A mix of sadness, frustration, and embarrassment melded inside her. "I don't know. I guess I'll go make an announcement that the concert is cancelled."

"Well, what are you going to tell them?"

"I don't know. I'll think of something." She headed for the stage and left Meredith standing with a look of devastation on her face. It was too hard to look her mother in the eye and know that she herself had caused this mess.

Avery had no one to blame but herself.

Shane pulled his car into the golf course entrance and glanced at his watch. The show was scheduled to start in five minutes; he was going to be late to his own concert. He'd forgotten about the parade in town, and he hadn't anticipated the line of traffic that was backed all the way from town to the resort. Luckily, he knew he could park at the golf course and jog the rest of the way.

He could see the stage set up on one of the greens, and he could hear the crowd rumbling in anticipation. Avery probably thought he wasn't coming, and he had no way to reach her. He had tried calling the resort but the line was busy. He had to get up to the stage, and quickly.

When he finally reached the back of the stage, he saw three figures standing in jeans and black leather jackets. He let out a sigh of relief. He'd only come up with this plan last night, but even on such short notice, the guys hadn't let him down.

"You guys made it!" he said, leaning in for a group hug.

"*You* made it. We thought we'd have to go on without ya," Sulley said with a grin.

"Did anyone get a chance to talk to James?" Shane asked, glancing again at his watch.

"No, but I called Lori. She's holding the jet for us until six. That will put us in New York by eight, then we'll go live on *The Aftershow* at ten. We're cutting it close, but it will all work out." Axel gave him a wink.

"I appreciate you guys coming, but you should know, James said if I put on this concert the label is dropping me. I can go on by myself and just do acoustics like I'd planned. You guys shouldn't take the heat for this."

"If you go down, we all go down together," Sulley said.

"There's no Distant Union without you, Shane. If they drop you, they're dropping all of us," Jax added.

Shane smiled, and the band hugged once more.

"I hate to break this up, but I need you guys on stage," the stagehand called out to them.

And in unison, Distant Union headed for side stage, ready to put on the best concert ever to come to Arbor Shores.

Avery started to make her way through the crowd but it was standing room only, and she could barely see the stage over the sea of people before her.

"Ladies and gentlemen, please put your hands together for

the one and only, Shane Knox, and his band, Distant Union!"
She stopped dead in her tracks. Was she hearing things?

She still couldn't see the stage, but the crowd was going
wild. Did this mean Shane was here? Hopefully the MC checked
for Shane before he announced his presence, because as far as
she knew, Shane hadn't showed.

"How are you doing this afternoon, Arbor Shores? Happy
Fourth of July!" She closed her eyes and exhaled for the first
time all day at the sound of Shane's voice. *Thank goodness.*
She'd never felt such a sense of relief in all of her life. She took
a minute to take in the sound of his guitar as he started to strum.

"Folks," he talked to the crowd as he strummed a single
cord. "I'd like to dedicate this first song to the woman who made
all of this possible. And I'd like to thank the Cooke family for
having me here today. Is this resort beautiful, or what?" The
crowd erupted.

He continued to strum. "For those of you who don't know, I
was born and raised here in Arbor Shores, and I spent many a
summer here at the resort with the Cooke family. Dax, my best
friend, Meredith and her late husband, Sal, who were like
parents to me, but mostly, the one girl I've never been able to get
over. The one I let get away long ago. The only girl I've ever
truly loved, Miss Avery Cooke."

The crowd erupted again, and Avery could feel heat rushing
to her cheeks.

"If I can have Avery come up here on stage, I'd like to dedicate this first song to her. Anyone see Avery Cooke out there?"
He stood up off the stool and scanned the audience.

"Here she is!" Rylee yelled out, and the crowd parted as they
all turned to watch her next move. Should she go up there? What
was he doing?

"Go up there, girl! What are you waitin' for?" A woman put
her hand on Avery's back and gave her a gentle nudge toward
the stage.

Avery could see Shane now, standing on the stage in his

black T-shirt and faded blue jeans, his guitar strapped across his chest. They locked eyes and Shane held out his hand to motion he was waiting for her to join him. She made her way to the stage, and he walked over to meet her by the stairs. As she approached the top, he took her hand and guided her over to the stool. He motioned for her to take a seat as he stood and adjusted the microphone.

"I'm going to play a special song for you, folks. This is one you've never heard before, because I just wrote it for this special girl right here."

The crowd went wild. Shane's voice echoed through the mic and out through the speakers. Avery looked up into his eyes, and he turned to face her as he sang.

Time slipped away with every lyric. She heard some of the words, but there was an unspoken language going on between their eyes. For once, there was no more guessing if he loved her, there was no more guessing if he was the one, there was no more wondering if she could trust him. His eyes said it all, and in that moment, something inside told her he'd never leave her again.

As the song came to an end, Shane sang the final verse.

You captured my heart a long time ago ...
Avery, girl, I promise, this time ...
I will never, ever let you go ...

The crowd erupted as he put down his guitar and helped her to her feet. He pulled her close and cupped her face in both hands. "Avery Cooke, I love you, and I promise I will never leave your side."

Avery nodded her head in approval, as if to give him permission, and Shane leaned his head down and placed his lips on hers. The crowd rose to their feet and continued to clap and cheer. Shane wrapped his arms tightly around her waist. He raised her up and swung her around, ending the moment with a long embrace as he whispered in her ear, "Tell me you'll give me another chance to show you what you mean to me? Tell me you feel it, too?" He pulled back and looked into her eyes, awaiting her response.

Avery swallowed hard. She'd never been so happy as she was in this moment. There was nothing she wanted more than to have Shane back in her life forever, and he'd just declared his love to her in front of thousands of people.

"I do, Shane. I never stopped. Not even for a minute."

The concert was a great success. Shane's energy was on fire as soon as he'd gotten his girl back. He looked over and Avery was standing off to the side of the stage now, watching the show with his brothers. Everything had come full circle. His father's heart attack was tragic, but it had somehow brought him back together with his family, even if they still had some work to do. It even brought Avery and Hunter together. Being on stage with his band —playing what they wanted to play instead of what they were told to play—he'd never felt more alive. He decided in that moment, from then on, he'd only play music on his own terms. Not because he was contracted to. He had a feeling his band felt the same way.

Shane wasn't sure what the future held for his career, but at least he'd found a way to put on the concert, make it to *The Aftershow*, and most importantly, get the girl.

One thing he was certain of as he looked out over the crowd on this beautiful summer day, Shane Knox was staying in Arbor Shores for good.

He would never leave his Avery again.

EPILOGUE

*H*unter Knox watched his brother on stage in admiration. He'd always looked up to Shane, but he'd never told him that. That's why he'd always had a love-hate relationship with his brother. On one hand, he wanted to impress his father and make Carter happy. Hunter loved that he was his father's favorite. On the other hand, he wished he'd had the opportunity to travel and enjoy his youth, and he didn't feel he had any of the talents Shane possessed.

With his father's health on the line, he wasn't sure what the future would hold. Carter had a long road of recovery ahead of him, and Hunter would probably need to step up even more in the family business to take some of the burden off of his father, but he didn't mind. He loved Knox Enterprises just as much as his father did, if not more. Still, he hoped his brother would stick around for a while. Though from the looks of Shane and Avery, he doubted his big brother would be going anywhere.

Hunter watched as Shane pulled Avery back out on stage before the last song, and got down on one knee in front of the crowd and proposed. She was quick to say yes, and they embraced before looking at each other with love in their eyes and sealing their engagement with a kiss.

Would he ever feel that way about someone? And would anyone ever feel that kind of love for him? That was something else Shane had that Hunter didn't, and he longed for it. Hunter sure had the looks, as did all of the Knox boys, and women came onto him all the time. Sure, he'd dated here and there, but work was always his number one priority. He always had something to prove to his father—he lived to make Carter proud. For that reason, relationships fizzled as quickly as they started. No woman had ever been able to hold his attention.

But now, watching Shane and Avery, Hunter was beginning to think he was ready for more.

Was it time for him to finally find a love of his own? And if he did fall in love, would he be able to balance a relationship with the demands of his career?

Couldn't he find some way to have it all?

Discover if Hunter finds true love. Read *Book Two* of the *Knox Brothers of Arbor Shores* series, *Captivating the Heart of the Billionaire.*

ABOUT THE AUTHOR

Nomi Summers is a clean contemporary romance author with a flair for taming bad boy heroes readers swoon over.

When she's not dreaming up her next small town romance, you'll find her at the beach devouring the latest new release on her Kindle. Her other guilty pleasures include getting lost in mindless reality TV and spending far too much time talking to her dogs, as she's convinced they understand every other word!

Nomi's living her own "happily ever after" with her loving husband and their two fur babies in Tampa Bay, Florida. However, a piece of her heart will always belong in Michigan where she's originally from—the inspiration behind the settings in her novels.

www.nomisummers.com

www.ingramcontent.com/pod-product-compliance
Lightning Source LLC
Chambersburg PA
CBHW071121100726
47908CB00008B/2449